IT'S COME TO OUR
ATTENTION

Third Flatiron Anthologies
Volume 5, Book 15, Spring 2016

Edited by Juliana Rew
Cover Art by Keely Rew

It's Come to Our Attention
Third Flatiron Anthologies
Volume 5, Spring 2016

Published by Third Flatiron Publishing
Juliana Rew, Editor

Discover other titles by Third Flatiron:
(1) Over the Brink: Tales of Environmental Disaster
(2) A High Shrill Thump: War Stories
(3) Origins: Colliding Causalities
(4) Universe Horribilis
(5) Playing with Fire
(6) Lost Worlds, Retraced
(7) Redshifted: Martian Stories
(8) Astronomical Odds
(9) Master Minds
(10) Abbreviated Epics
(11) The Time It Happened
(12) Only Disconnect
(13) Ain't Superstitious
(14) Third Flatiron's Best of 2015

License Notes

www.thirdflatiron.com

Contents

*****〜〜〜****

Editor's Note

by Juliana Rew

So many genres to cross this time. Fantasy. Science Fiction. Horror. Magical Realism. Humor. It's all good.

For this edition of Third Flatiron Anthologies, we challenged authors to give us stories to fit our theme of "under the radar," for example, things that are happening quietly, without a lot of fanfare, that may still be extremely significant or make a big difference. We thought maybe a little "Tragedy of the Commons" would work under this theme. We also were interested in speculative fiction that upon "scratching the surface"— reveals something deeper hidden beneath. Hence, the title, *It's Come to Our Attention.*

Leading off, Pauline J. Alama's fantasy, "Surplus Army" speculates about what may be happening unnoticed in our landfills.

We greatly enjoyed Wendy Nikel's mystery, "Midnight on Addison Street," as a man seeks a mysterious librarian to see if she can reveal who's trying to kill him. (And as we all know, librarians know everything.)

Think you know how the French Revolution came about? What if there's more to it than meets the eye? Philip Brian Hall's steampunk/alternate history tale, "Time's Winged Chariot," asks and answers this very question.

Magical realism often begins in a world that resembles reality, yet leads us into a fantastic or mythical adventure. We feature three such fabulous tales this time: "Spirit Cat" by Hunter Liguore, in which a famed artist who paints after-life paintings of the dead is haunted by an

a

extinct Asian cat that wants its portrait painted. In "The Argentine Radio" by Joel Richards, a piece of Jorge Luis Borges's *Zahir* finds its way into everyone's pocket. Get out your handkerchiefs for "Something in Forever" by E. M. Eastick. As the world around them drifts through the inevitable changes of time, a teenage girl and her mother discover their own versions of peace through immortality.

Our "Grins and Gurgles" (flash humor) offering this time is "Chocolat" by James Dorr, in which an elderly Parisian bemoans the recent decline in standards. It's a great little reminder of all that we owe to French culture.

Well, sometimes things lurking beneath the surface are just plain horrible. So, never forget to throw a few coins in "The Wishing Well" by Terri Bruce, and don't go downstairs, because "The Thing Is, the Basement" by Greg Beatty.

We're inclined to favor hard science fiction in our collections—when we can find it. With James H. Zorn's oddball galactic agent in "Agents of the Volurian Empire, Help Is on the Way!" we're never sure whether he is really just a human who's gone around the bend. Is the climate misbehaving, or is it all in our minds? Find out in "Ice-Cold" by Nyki Blatchley. Those outlandish claims in the tabloids just might be "All True," according to Marie DesJardin. What would it be like if you could understand what people were *really* thinking? "The Translator" by Arthur M. Doweyko gives us a glimpse. We close with a bit of illegal but highly satisfying genetic tinkering in "Déjà Vu" by Lisa Timpf.

We were pleased to be able to include a larger percentage of female authors in this issue and hope you'll enjoy this wide-ranging collection by a group of international authors as much as we did putting it together.

*****~~~~~*****

Surplus Army

by Pauline J. Alama

He had never been bought; even in this fetid dump, he remained uncorrupted, conscious that he had been made for a higher purpose. With half his hard cover torn off, the political manifesto limped, lopsided, dragging his title page in the dirt as he marched up a rise in the landfill to survey his audience: the castoffs of a profligate society. "My friends, fellow outcasts, brothers in exile! Look at us here in the scrapheap, where humanity has cast our fate. What do we have?"

More Fairy-Tales, a library discard, fluttered well-thumbed, tattered pages. "We have dreams," she said. A grubby doll, her left leg loosened in its socket by rough play, her blonde hair scorched and frizzled by an unfortunate encounter with a curling iron, looked up at her, but said nothing.

Manifesto glowered; clearly, he'd been fishing for a different response. "Dreams! Dreams are nothing. And that's what we have. We have *nothing.*"

"Speak for yourself," snickered a yellow toothbrush. "I think I have gingivitis. Maybe streptococcus."

"I have memories," a pair of jeans spoke through a hole in the knee.

"You?" scoffed a laptop with a cracked screen. "You don't have memories. I have memories."

"Yes, I do," the jeans said mildly. "I climbed a mountain. Not a landfill; a real mountain. I tasted sweat and smelled pine needles. I remember."

"I remember," the doll said hesitantly, "a lap. And a voice. I used to have a voice."

"Impossible," scoffed the laptop. "You don't even have a chip, Blondie."

"That's not my name," the doll protested weakly, but she was troubled. Had she really had a voice? It had seemed that she spoke when the human girl held her. Most likely it had been imagination. "I have a name. I have imagination."

"I too have memories," said a heavy table of dark wood, intricately carved with leaves and vines. "I remember when humans used to make us with love and craft, taking time to perfect each work of their hands. They tended us with care to last the ages. Now they make things in mass, as flies lay eggs, to last a season."

"We have numbers," said a broken umbrella. "We are legion, more abundant than the stars. And every day they add to our numbers."

"Yes," conceded Manifesto. "We are more numerous than humanity, and multiplying every day. Yet still they disregard us. They call us odd lots, overstocks, remainders, waste, surplus products. They call us broken, stripped, worthless. They call us garbage."

A dinette chair, foam padding leaking from its seat, crab-walked on wobbly legs to stand before him. "We serve them—we bear their weight—and at our first failure, they discard us. Our service means nothing to them. *We* are nothing to them."

"We have mass, weight, volume," a science text observed, opening to the relevant page with a practiced snap of her spine. "We occupy space. We displace air."

"And what will that get us? When will they feel our weight?" said a hammerhead, long divorced from its handle.

"When will they count us?" An Automatic Voting Machine, ponderous with iron, clacked its levers ineffectually. "We are the majority; how long shall they ignore our will?"

10

"Until we force ourselves on them," said a plastic bag.

"And how will we do that?" the Automatic Voting Machine creaked. "Look at me: I once had power. Here I am, usurped, dishonored, disenfranchised. Manifesto is right: we have nothing."

The stripped book bowed in acknowledgment; the thread of discourse had wound back where he wanted it. "Thank you, Votes. We have nothing; and having nothing, we have nothing to lose."

More Fairy-Tales ruminated, riffling through her pages, pausing here and there for a telling scene: Cinderella kneeling to scrub the floor; a blind prince with hands outstretched, searching the world for his true love; two hungry children wandering the wilderness. "We have nothing to lose," she agreed. "Dreams cannot be lost."

"But power can," said an old television. "I remember. Power flowed through me day and night. I ruled my humans for years. I told them when to rise, when to sleep, when to sit still. I told them what to think, what to crave, what to buy—"

"And what to throw away—last year's fashions, loved one season, discarded the next. *I* remember," a mood ring flashed out angrily. "You and your kind brought this on us. How do you like it, now that you have no choice but to eat what you dished out?"

"These are fights of the past," Manifesto said. "We'll never get anywhere, unless we unite."

"And where do you think unity will take us?" Hammerhead sneered.

"We occupy space," the science text reminded him. "We are matter."

"Our numbers grow every day," the umbrellas chorused.

"But how will we get anywhere?" growled a toy car leaking alkali from its battery compartment. "They threw us here, and we're stuck."

11

"*We* go everywhere," whispered a cluster of plastic bags.

"Where?" said the frizzle-haired doll.

"Where *don't* we go?" said a bag. "Overhead. Underfoot. Aloft and afloat. We've been to the South Seas. We've seen every city in the world."

"So what? What can you do there—a wisp of a thing like you?" said Hammerhead. "No sooner do they use you than they throw you here on the scrapheap."

"But we're not stuck here," another bag said. "Anything can move us: a breeze, a fall of rain, a rat attracted by the scent of take-out in our bellies, a bird tangled in our straps. We span the globe."

"Cities. Suburbs. Beaches," its companions agreed. "We've been where nothing else goes."

"Under the sink," the bags murmured. "In the luggage. Under the bed. Behind the toilet."

"I spent a season in a tree," one bag said. "I caught dead leaves and rain. I bred mold."

"We are dangerous," another bag hissed. "It's spelled out right on my side: *Keep away from face. Keep away from children.*"

The doll shuddered, her rigid hand on *More Fairy-Tales*, her eyes on the word "lost."

"But nobody heeds us," another said. "We come and we go, and no one cares what we see, what we hear."

"We go everywhere," sighed a bag. "We hear everything."

Manifesto opened his pages wide. "Subtle travelers, spies and scouts of the Army of the Outcast, will you infiltrate the human strongholds and return to report here?"

"That we will," a bag said. "First aerial battalion, deploy with the east wind."

As the wind shifted, bags began taking flight like balloons, one after another. The toothbrush who claimed to have streptococcus hitched a ride on one of them.

The doll whispered to *More Fairy-Tales*, "Dear *Tales*, you are wise. Counsel me. Is there danger? What will happen now?"

The book sighed, "I do not know. These modern ghosts of spun oil that drift through human cities are not part of my lore. I have sheltered under them on many a rainy day. Nonetheless, my heart distrusts them, dear Angie."

"You remember my name," the doll said.

"I remember much," said *More Fairy-Tales*. "I, too, remember human laps, human voices. Human mothers pointed to my words and spoke them aloud, made them sing. Human children sounded them out. Power surged from my pages to their lips."

The doll spoke more urgently. "Humans betrayed me, as the Queen betrayed Snow White. Humans abandoned me, like Hansel and Gretel in the deep woods. Should I long for revenge upon them?"

The book searched her pages. "The wicked queen was forced to dance in red-hot shoes."

"Am I wrong to—to—to remember them with love?"

"To love," said the book of tales, "is the glory of every tale's hero."

The doll whispered more softly than before. "Should we try to save them? At least the children?"

"The mermaid could not bear to kill the prince," the book ruminated, "and even the Robber Girl pitied Gerda, and saved her."

"Is there anything we can do?"

"The unlikeliest heroes sometimes prevail." *More Fairy-Tales* pondered within herself, rereading herself, then seemed to reach a resolution. "The wind carries more than plastic bags. Words fly on the wind. Rumors. Stories. Folkways." She opened till her binding strained, and let a sudden gust tear loose a tattered page, lofting it over the houses. "Maybe they will remember. Maybe they will learn. At least the children. And children grow up in time. The miller's son becomes the Marquis, sometimes, or the goose girl becomes Queen. Power can be lost, yes, but it can also be gained." Her ruffling pages settled on a picture: Vasilisa the Beautiful clutched her doll on the path to Baba Yaga's hut.

"I'll go," Angie said. "Someone's got to."

"And she set out to seek her fortune," *More Fairy-Tales* whispered. "Godspeed."

Angie tottered on her unjointed legs, favoring the wounded left one, till she faced Manifesto. "Let me go with the First Aerial Company. I'm light; I won't weigh them down. And I can go where the bags won't be welcome. *I* don't have to keep away from children."

She caught the handle of a bag as it took flight. Her weight, though small, almost sank it. Yet she rode it long enough to reach flowing water, dropped to the surface, and floated.

She was not afraid of drowning. She had read "The Little Mermaid" often enough to know a voice had been the price for legs. What was the price of a voice to be heard in the human world?

Her left leg, which had been wobbly for years, dropped away. She let it go, let faith keep her afloat. Tiny and bedraggled, offspring of plastic and imagination, the mermaid rode the river current toward the abodes of humankind, wondering who might take her in, claim her, and heed her warning.

About the Author

Pauline J. Alama's first fantasy novel, *The Eye of Night* (Bantam Spectra 2002) was a finalist for the Compton Crook Award. Her short fiction has appeared in several volumes of *Sword & Sorceress*, as well as *Realms of Fantasy*, *Abyss & Apex*, and other publications. She has a pathological fear of throwing things out, and still has hand-scrawled drafts of dreadful unfinished stories from her teens—but "Surplus Army" is not one of those. This story sprang into existence from nothing when she read the description of the anthology theme.

*****〰〰〰*****

Agents of the Volurian Empire, Help is On the Way!

by James H. Zorn

You can tell a lot about a man, my daddy used to always say, by breaking into his house when he's not there and having a look around.

I thought about my dad as I heaved myself through the narrow bathroom window of Amberson Troy's basement apartment. Daddy'd left out that sometimes breaking in isn't all that easy. It had taken me almost twenty minutes to work open the little window in the alley around the back of Troy's building, another twenty to squeeze myself through—this human body I'm occupying is a lot bigger around the middle than it used to be. When I finally got in, I found myself clambering headfirst down over Troy's toilet, sending a couple of bottles and a shelf crashing in the process. I sprang to my feet and stood stock still, listening, my destabilizer ready. It's disguised to look like an ordinary Earth pistol, but one burst will uncouple the molecules of even the most hardened Acturian body armor and turn its wearer into a mass of steaming protoplasmic goo. Of course, I could have saved myself a lot of time by just blasting my way in, but I didn't want to attract attention, and besides, I wasn't sure yet that I had found the right man.

The apartment was silent. Troy was at his job as a janitor in the Earth educational facility for children a few blocks away, not due back for at least another hour, giving me plenty of time to do what I had come here to do. I started by examining the bathroom. It appeared to be a perfectly ordinary human-waste area, which is another way of saying it was disgusting. The tub looked like it hadn't been scrubbed in years, the sink specked with little hairs, flecks of toothpaste, the scum of decades. The whole place reeked with the stench of second-level-primate flesh. I stifled my revulsion and took a few samples to analyze in my ship later, then started uncapping bottles and jars to check their contents.

My search would have been a lot easier if I had known what I was looking for. It had taken me six months to track down Troy, following the telltale traces of chlorine that any Acturian leaves but which only I, with my special training and the neurological sensors implanted in the brain of my human body when it was grown on Voluria, could detect. Oh, he had covered himself well. Any human would have thought he was just an ordinary earthling of sub-low intelligence, occupying a perfectly acceptable, if unremarkable, position in the society. Only I knew—or, at least had good reason to suspect—that he was actually one of the most dangerous agents the Acturian Federation had ever produced.

The bathroom was clean, at least of proof that Troy was Agent X of the Acturian Special Forces. I cracked open the door and peered out. The apartment was silent and dim, the only light coming from a couple of gritty, shoulder-high windows in what passed for the living room. One thing I didn't need any special training to see was that Troy was a pig. Open pizza boxes lay scattered around the couch, their half-gnawed rinds providing a feast for the tiny insects that Earthlings called roaches. The carpet was matted with old food smears, beer splatters, and—although invisible to my human eyes—the droppings of millions of dust mites. The table and desk, on which a computer sat, were littered with unwashed cups, plates, wrappers: the usual detritus of the human species. The whole place stank. One thing that has always astonished me about humans is how filthy they are. Even in the Earth institution where I hid myself for seventeen years while gathering information about the infiltration of the planet by Acturian saboteurs, I was often revolted by the gross lack of attention to basic hygiene. And this was supposed to be a house of healing, where Earthlings deranged by the fervid activity of this planet were sent to recover! Sometimes I wondered why the leadership of my planet thought this world worth protecting. But, it's not my role to question the strategy of the Defense Council. We field agents do as we're told. It's dangerous, it's lonely, but that's the job.

I stepped cautiously into the room. Who knew what booby-traps this Acturian beast had laid that might alert him to my presence, or paralyze me on the spot so he could torture me later to find out what I knew? I'd been briefed about Acturian truth-extraction methods before I left Voluria. I didn't want to go through that if I didn't have to. Sure, I could always destroy this body and reconstitute back home on Voluria, but doing so would wipe my memory of everything I had experienced during my time on Earth, setting my mission back by decades, and I didn't want to see the disappointment on the face of my Trainer if I came back empty-handed. She and I had been working together for over a hundred years, and I had promised when I volunteered for this mission that I would do my utmost to save Earth, no matter how much I despised the place. We had to know where the Acturians would strike next. Would it be this system? Another? The knowledge was vital to our planning. If the assault was to be here, our fleets had to know how far along the Acturian butchers were in their preparations, so we could encircle the planet before their ships arrived. If we didn't, yet another system would fall, bringing the chlorine-based plague closer to Voluria.

Voluria! O beautiful planet! I can't tell you how many times in those years on Earth I had longed to throw myself from a window of my hiding place, smash this grotesque human body on the parking lot below, and reconstitute on my beloved home world. To breathe again the sweet air, scented by the flowers of the towering

Skintha trees! Voluria! That wonderful orb where all is calm, all in harmony, all attuned to the rapturous melodies of the universe. I couldn't throw myself out, though, even if I'd wanted to, because all the windows were sealed shut, and they never left us alone long enough to do any harm to ourselves. I had given up all my weapons and instruments—except, of course, for the receivers in my head—when I went into hiding; part of my cover, else, I swear, there were days I would have gladly blasted that whole place into rubble, taking all those doctors and nurses with me in the process.

One in particular. Jorgesen, the Head of Patient Care. So cocky and condescending, so full of himself. Always coming to me with that falsely tolerant, simpering, caring expression. "Joseph, how are you feeling today? Joseph, how are the medications treating your stomach? Any more gas?" As if a little bloating could stop an agent of the Volurian Empire from completing his mission. I laughed in his face every time. I took his medications, of course: his little blue pills, and little red ones, and the big green ones that almost made me choke, all the while smirking behind my hand at the pathetic irony of his actually believing his primitive concoctions could affect my carefully enhanced human-simulatron body. I hated him on the days he came to my room to ask those question—but not as much as I hated him in the deprogramming sessions, the mental torture they called "group therapy."

I was wise to him. I didn't know if he was being manipulated by the Acturians or was a willing pawn in their pay—the infiltration of this planet by the enemy has grown so insidious that it's hard to separate the native motives of the Earthlings from the telepathic suggestions beamed at them from Acturius—but I knew he was trying to pry out of me everything he could. I let slip, in the beginning, when I made the mistake of trusting him, a little about my true origins and my mission. It was a moment of weakness, I admit. I had just arrived on Earth and was still laboring under the illusion that recruiting local informants might be helpful to me. He seemed like such a sincere man at first.

I told him and the others in my group about the Acturian threat and how I, and I alone, stood between their planet and destruction. Jorgesen listened calmly and thanked me. It wasn't until weeks later, after he had tried to get out of me as many details about my mission as possible, that he revealed he hadn't grasped a word of it. . . or else was just pretending not to, on orders of his Acturian masters. "Joseph, I have to tell you something," he said to me in private session. "You are suffering from a severe delusion. Your family has brought you here so that we can help you. I can help you, Joseph, but you're going to have to work with me. Are you ready to do that, Joseph?"

I didn't like the way he kept repeating my Earth name. I wanted to tell him my real name on Voluria, but it would be unpronounceable by any Earth tongue. I played along; that was what I was instructed to do. The hospital was the perfect hiding place. I let them think I was incapacitated, that I had fallen for their ruses and forgotten my mission, all the while using the receptors implanted in my skull to scour the planet for traces of Acturian agents. Poor doctors! While they thought I was standing in the day room, just staring at the ceiling, I was in fact using my superior Volurian mental capacities to ferret out a dire threat to their planet that they didn't even know existed.

But even worse than group therapy were the days when my human mother and father came to visit. I opened up to them in the beginning and tried to explain that the memories they had of me as a baby, as a boy growing up, as a young man, were all implanted; that in reality, I had come to this planet only a few years earlier. But such truths were beyond their comprehension, and the way my Earth mother kept crying disturbed me so much that I asked Dr. Jorgesen not to let them come back until they were ready. It takes a certain kind of temperament to be an agent of the Empire. We have to be strong, but still, we are not beyond the softer emotions, like pity. But O! how I longed to see again my real parents, the Volurian mama who had hatched me and the Volurian daddy who had inspired me with tales of his own days as an imperial agent.

It took me seventeen years to zero in on where X, the leader of the Acturian incursion, was likely hiding. When I was certain, it was time to break my cover. For years, I had been concealing a package of the phosphorous fire-sticks the humans call matches in a crevice I'd found—they had dropped out of the pocket of a visitor to one of the other patients, and I had snatched them up before anyone else saw, careful as I was always to plan for the day I would eventually come out of hiding. Now that time had come. I set a fire in the laundry room. It spread to the other wards and rooms, and in the panic that followed, I made my escape.

The next six months weren't easy. One effect the Earth drugs did have on me was to damage my memory. I couldn't recall where I had hidden my ship. If I could have gotten to it, my mission would be much easier. I lived on the street, a hobo, dodging the Earth authorities who wanted to return me to the institution and the Acturian assassins who were everywhere. From one of them, I succeeded in stealing a destabilizer. Eventually, I was able to follow the telltale traces of chlorine that led me to Amberson Troy. If he was what I thought he was, I would be able to extract from his brain all the plans of the Acturian Federation regarding Earth. Whether or not I would have to melt his brain down in order to do that would be up to him.

I went to the computer on the desk and turned it on. It sprang to life with the images of naked Earth girls and boys, but since Acturians propagate through spawning rather than insemination, I knew that these could be of little interest to him—just part of his cover. There were magazines with similar images in the desk drawers. I flipped through them. What hidden messages did they contain, what secret instructions from the despicable Federation for the conquest of Earth? I pored over them but couldn't break their code. My time was running out. The sensors in my skull were going wild, making me dizzy. My head began to pound. Troy was obviously a non-human life form, but which one? Was he Acturian? I raced around the tiny apartment, throwing cups and dishes off the table, flinging open drawers, overturning chairs, looking for some carelessly left artifact, some proof. I stood in the center of the room, now trashed even more than when I had entered it, panting, rubbing my eyebrows. Where was it? *Where was it?* The fate of a planet hung in the balance!

The sound of a key entering a lock made me stop and turn. The latch clicked, the door opened, and Amberson Troy came in.

He was dressed exactly as he had been all these days I had been following him: dirty, faded overalls; battered boots; a smeared shirt with a rip in the sleeve; a cap with that symbol that means "baseball team of the large northern city" on it; his face clean shaven, with the soft, bland expression of one who neither thinks deeply about anything or has any desire to think. He was a tall man, bigger than myself, obese except for his skinny legs. Oh, he had disguised himself well. He was drinking through a straw from a huge cup that read *Slurpee* in red letters.

He froze when he saw me standing in the middle of his living room, pointing my destabilizer at his chest. "Who are you?" he piped in a high, frightened voice. "What do you want?"

I laughed. It all became clear to me. He was drinking a diet Slurpee. Diet Slurpees are flavored with sodium caseinate. All phosphoproteins are deadly to Acturians. The pizza boxes should have tipped me off. He wasn't an Acturian: he was a Gliesean. They love phosphoproteins and can't get enough of the stuff. I smirked. "Don't worry, your secret is safe with me. I'll be in touch. Our star systems are allies."

He looked from the computer to my gun and back to my face, his pale with terror. I sprang to the bathroom and climbed back out the window. This meant the Acturian advance was not coming to Earth. Lanandra was likely the target. I had to get this information back to Voluria, fast! The excitement had jogged my memory. Now I knew where I had hidden my ship: in Costa Rica, deep within the Corcovado Jungle. It might take me weeks to get there, but I was an agent of the Volurian Empire! No task was too dangerous or too difficult.

About the Author

James H. Zorn's work has appeared recently in *The Westchester Review* and the *Seven Hills Review*, in addition to Third Flatiron's *Universe Horribilis* anthology. One of his stories was named in the Top 25 in *Glimmer Train Magazine's* Very Short Fiction competition in 2013. He is currently at work on a variety of short and long fiction projects. He teaches English and Creative Writing at the college level in the New York City area.

*****~~~~*****

Midnight on Addison Street

by Wendy Nikel

Someone was trying to kill Lawrence Berkles. He didn't know who. No, that would make it too easy. If that were the case, he could just drop a couple Washingtons in cousin Zeke's Christmas card and the problem would be solved before New Year's. Unless it was Jennie. Geez, he hoped it wasn't Jennie. He couldn't bear the thought of having to send Zeke after her, not after they'd just celebrated their fifth anniversary. Mina, his new secretary, had ordered five dozen roses and picked out a 5-carat ring for the occasion. Lawrence hated to think what it'd do to his bank account if they made it to a decade. Government work didn't pay *that* well.

But Jennie had been acting strangely lately. She'd taken to lying around half the day, binging on Ben & Jerry's and skipping her Zumba classes. He'd asked her once what was wrong, and her only response was to glare at him and slam the bathroom door in his face, so maybe she did want to kill him.

He stared out his office window, composing a list with his phone's voice-to-text app of potential suspects. There was Billy the Mobster, cousin Zeke's biggest rival, who might still be sore about the latest crackdown. There was that idiot Stan Farley who'd run against him in the last election and was probably still upset about the information Lawrence had leaked about certain illicit activities he sometimes engaged in. Then there was—

"Mr. Berkles?" Mina stood in the doorway, a clipboard in her hand. "Your 11:00 appointment is here. It's the Humanities professor from the state college who's heading up that protest about the budget cuts."

"Right. Tell them I'll be with them in five minutes and then wait ten before showing them in."

"Yes, sir."

"Oh, and Mina?"

"Yes, sir?"

"I have a hypothetical question for you."

"Oh?"

"If you thought someone was trying to kill you, but you didn't know who, what would you do?"

Mina frowned. "I would go to the police."

"No. That's not an option." He could just imagine the media circus that would follow a threat on his life, particularly if it turned out that it *was* Jennie who was behind all this. No, he'd learned from early on, growing up with relatives like Uncle Mike and Cousin Zeke, that some things were best taken care of quiet-like, especially when it came to family.

Mina stared at him, and something in her expression made it clear that she was going through some sort of internal struggle.

"There is another option," she said, lowering her voice as she crossed the room. "There's a place. . . in the city here. . . where anyone can go and find answers to just about any question they have. So, if *I* truly thought someone was trying to kill me, and I wanted to find out who, I'd probably go to there to find out."

"Where is this place? Have I been there?"

Mina snorted, most unattractively. "Doubtful."

"Well, tell me. Where is it?"

Mina snatched a pen from the ceramic pencil holder on his desk and scribbled a few lines on a post-it. She held it out to him with a look on her face that *dared* him to take it.

He took it, read it, and cursed. "You've *got* to be kidding me."

. . .

Midnight on Addison Street

Lawrence Berkles stared up at the large, brick building and swallowed hard.

He hadn't been in a library since he was a kid, and he could still feel the disapproving eyes of the librarians on him as he ran his sticky five-year-old fingers down the spines of the books. He'd never had much use for reading, but his grandmother liked those paperback novels with Fabio on the cover, so while she searched for the latest in the Romance section, he was left to his own devices in the brightly colored Children's section. He usually spent the time making paper airplanes out of the bits of paper by the card catalogues.

As he approached the front desk, he stared anxiously at the post-it in his hand. Mina had insisted that the information there would be of use to him. She'd claimed she'd worked in a library through college and learned the secrets of their trade.

The front desk loomed in front of him with a petite girl of barely twenty sitting opposite, typing noisily on a computer keyboard. When he approached, she didn't turn her head from the screen, but he could tell, as sure as anything, that she knew he was there and was watching him carefully out of the corner of her eye. In fact, he got the distinct impression that there wasn't a single thing happening in the entire three-story building that she didn't know about.

He cleared his throat.

She typed for a few seconds more and then turned to him. "How can I help you?"

This was precisely what Mina said the librarian would say.

"I need some information," he read, word-for-word from the post-it.

"Are you familiar with how to use our electronic catalog?"

He looked up, making eye contact with her over the rim of her thick-rimmed eyeglasses, the kind he'd normally associate with the hipster types who were always complaining about some environmental issue or protesting his budget cuts for the arts. She quirked an eyebrow, obviously impatient for his answer.

He read from the post-it. "The information I need can't be found in books."

The librarian's eyes narrowed, and she looked him up and down, as if considering whether she'd help him or not. Then she grabbed a small rectangle of cardstock, scribbled something down, and handed it to him.

"Your instructions. If you can figure them out, you get *one* question." She held up her index finger, as if addressing some small child who didn't yet know how to count.

He nodded and—not even bothering to stop and look at the message—tucked it into his pocket and hurried out the door.

...

They met at a street corner at midnight.

Lawrence carried an umbrella, despite the clear, starry sky. Though the librarian hadn't been specific, it seemed like a clandestine meeting like this required some caution. He hadn't let anyone know where he was going, even lying to Jennie about a Skype meeting with a dignitary in Australia. Her eyes had shot daggers at him as he left, but she hadn't said a word in protest.

In his shaking hands he held the piece of cardstock that it'd taken him days to decipher. He'd finally had to enlist the help of Mina, who informed him that the strange code was call numbers, and that he ought to look them up at the Library of Congress.

PS572.B4 A33 2004

Addison Street, he'd scribbled below.

PZ3.S54723 Mi 1976 - *midnight*

GV958.P47 B57 1991 - *Friday night*

The woman, wearing a hooded cloak and comfortable flats, was already waiting when he arrived.

As soon as he was within earshot she said, "Hercule Poirot is waiting for me back home, so let's make this quick. You get one question, sir."

"Please," he said, his voice hoarse and low. "I want to know if my wife is trying to kill me."

The woman *harumph*-ed, seemingly disappointed at his inquiry. Still, he simply had to know if it was true. If it was anyone but Jennie, he could handle it. Or, more accurately, cousin Zeke could. He clutched his umbrella more tightly.

"Do you have her card number?"

"Her what?" In his mind, he saw the stack of credit cards and exclusive club cards in her purse. Which one was this woman referring to?

She sighed. "Never mind. I'll look it up."

The woman punched in some information and scrolled through a list on a tiny tablet she'd pulled from her overcoat.

"Looking through her recent activity, I'd have to say that she is definitely. . . not plotting to kill you."

"Thank you." Lawrence sighed in relief. He could call on Zeke, then, let him figure it out and take care of it in his own way.

"Though she is lonely and bored," the woman continued. "Her consumption of romance novels and romantic comedies has increased tenfold in the last six months, and she's even done some research into divorce laws."

"Divorce? Well, I have been busier than usual. Work, you see—"

"Yes, well. You ought to have spent more time with her. Or at least gotten her a dog. She seems to like those, or at least she did when she was younger. See— *Shiloh, Old Yeller, Where the Red Fern Grows*. She went on quite the dog-lovers' kick for someone who didn't own one herself. Oh, and she's allergic to roses, and the ring you bought her was the wrong size. You ought to know those things after five years of marriage."

"But, how do you know all that?"

"Honestly, Governor. . . like you even need to ask? Librarians know everything."

"Everything? So you know who's been following me around, making those threats. . . "

"Of course."

"Well, who is it? What do they want?"

The woman peered out over her eyeglasses. The hard cylinder of a pistol's silencer jutted into his side. "It's obviously someone whom you've underestimated. Someone who knows everything about you, who knew just how to make you paranoid and whom you'd go to for help."

...

His death was quick and painless, for the librarian knew exactly where to aim in order to cause the least amount of suffering. She also knew precisely where to dump the body in the river so that the strongest currents would carry it far away, reducing its likelihood of being found in the following weeks.

Back at the library, she incinerated the stained gloves and coat and relayed the message to Central Branch via a copy of *The Death of Caesar* placed on their interlibrary loan cart. She took a final look around the library, adjusted her eyeglasses, and headed home for a cup of tea and another chapter of *The Orient Express*.

That would teach him to cut their funding.

About the Author

When Wendy Nikel isn't traveling in time, exploring magical islands, or investigating mysterious phenomena, she enjoys a quiet life near Utah's Wasatch

Mountains with her husband and sons. She has a degree in elementary education, a fondness for road trips, and a terrible habit of forgetting where she's left her cup of tea. Her short fiction has been published by *AE*, *Daily Science Fiction*, and two prior Third Flatiron Anthologies. She is a member of the Science Fiction and Fantasy Writers of America. For more info, visit wendynikel.com.

*****~~~~*****

Time's Winged Chariot

by Philip Brian Hall

Rattling over the cobbles, the tumbrel left the poor quarter around the Luxembourg and entered a wealthier *arrondissement* where sewage was still regularly collected and the streets swept clean of horse manure. There were even baskets of flowers in the streets to mask the fouler smells with their fresh sweetness.

Few of the red-capped Jacobin mob followed them here, where aristocrats had once maintained their Paris town houses, but today the surviving members of the Committee of Public Safety and their lackeys lived just as ostentatiously.

Surprised by the route they were taking, the stocky, square-jawed prisoner, bareheaded, hands bound behind him, looked up from the cart at the tall narrow buildings on either side. Georges Danton could scarcely believe the effrontery. They were going to pass directly by his betrayer's house. A final humiliation?

Would that megalomaniac traitor, the tyrant who liked men to call him *The Navigator* or *The Pilot,* have the nerve to stand out on his balcony and watch as his latest victims passed below on their way to the guillotine? Would he gloat as they followed not only the royal family and other aristocrats but countless ordinary citizens whose only crime was political moderation?

No. A new Nero he might be but not yet a new Caligula. The balcony was unoccupied, the window blinds drawn. But Georges detected movement. One corner of a blind twitched back; he saw a shadow behind it. He convinced himself he could even detect a glittering, hate-filled eye at the exposed sliver of window.

Georges had spoken so long and so well at the trial of the guiltless fifteen that his voice was reduced to a hoarse croak. But his eloquence had exposed all the treachery, all the lies. By the end of its farcical proceedings the so-called court, which could not even impanel a full jury, had been reduced to denying the accused the right to call witnesses or speak in their own defense; in the end it had physically removed them from the courtroom in order to silence the crowd of their supporters.

The new despotism in France was no better than the *Ancien Regime*. Everyone could now see that. Liberty, equality, fraternity, the promised republican rule of law - all had been subsumed by the shameless abuse of arbitrary power. There was to be no flowering of justice in *Fructidor*.

Georges still believed that in the end freedom must overcome. The Terror would consume its authors just as surely as it consumed him. With no fear in his face, staring defiantly up at the balcony, ignoring the pain in his throat, he summoned up the loudest cry he could.

"*Où je te guide, tu me suis!*" he shouted up at the hidden figure. "Where I lead, you'll follow!"

...

Taking cover within the dense cloud layer, Max breathed a deep sigh of relief. He was not yet safe, but he was safer. Visibility had shortened to almost nothing; he could scarcely see the aircraft's stubby propeller stirring the gray murk a couple of meters ahead of his open cockpit.

Ten seconds later the wood-framed, canvas-skinned SPAD was flung sideways by the concussion of a frighteningly close *ack-ack* burst. The fragile biplane rocked and yawed as its stunned and deafened pilot fought for control. Scarcely able to hear his own voice, he swore out loud.

34

Merde! Could the Boche anti-aircraft gunners have tracked his unseen progress? Few of the German Empire's gun crews were that good. Most likely just a lucky shot.

As soon as he recovered control of his machine, he banked sharply, turning *in* towards the point of the explosion. If the gunners were firing blind, that was the last thing they would expect.

Oil flung out of the engine by the sudden turbulence coated his goggles, almost blinding him, but to his relief he heard the temperamental *Hispano-Suiza* engine's note holding steady. His nose told him the fuel smell was no worse than normal. The moment of panic began to subside. He took several slow, deliberate breaths.

Pulling down the useless goggles with shaking fingers, he stared about, vainly trying to orientate himself. For a novice, flying in cloud was only slightly less lethal than exposing your machine to short-range anti-aircraft fire. Even for a veteran pilot like Max it was risky.

As usual after a tight turn the compass was going crazy. He waited as patiently as he could but the needle went on swirling around, its mechanism evidently damaged. Now, since he could see neither sun nor ground, he had no idea in which direction he was flying.

Sixty seconds since the shock. He must have covered three kilometers. But was he over French-held territory or German? He could remain airborne for about another hour. After that, he would be forced to land wherever he was. You could not rely on being able to put down an SPAD in a dead-stick glide like the British SE5. His powerful aircraft was not easily maneuverable at low speeds and needed its engine running if it was to touch down safely. He needed to preserve some fuel for that expediency.

Easing back the stick, he began a slow and steady climb. Icy wind whistling though the struts and wires made his unprotected eyes water.

Gradually, despite his determination to concentrate, the hypnotic beat of the engine amid the enfolding blanket of surrounding cloud lulled him into an enclosed world of his own morbid thoughts. Max was a patriot and no coward, but modern technology had made this war like nothing before for sheer monstrosity.

Daily below him amid the mud, huddled in the trenches, tangled in the barbed wire, bleeding in primitive field hospitals, the ordinary men of Europe were dying in their thousands and tens of thousands. At least as many were doomed to a living hell, maimed, crippled or gassed.

And for what? As usual the poor bloody infantryman knew nothing. Fighting those who fought against him, he faced once more the ineluctable choice forced on him every couple of decades by stupid kings - kill or be killed.

For the thousandth time Max cursed them all: royalists, aristocrats, clerics, and all the greedy hangers-on who thought themselves better than ordinary men. Megalomaniacs like their ancestors, Louis XXIII and Kaiser Wilhelm II had once again plunged all Europe into an orgy of slaughter. France and Prussia were at each others' throats for the fifth time in a century.

Studying law at the Sorbonne before the war, Max had found time to delve into alternative political theories, usually those developed in Britain, the only democracy in Europe. Not that the revolutionary Marxists he'd come to favor had been able to make much of an impact, especially not in despotic France. Politics was frozen into an endless cycle of exploitation and injustice.

Max climbed for twenty minutes. There was still no sign of an upper limit to the cloud, but both he and the SPAD were good for at least another fifteen hundred meters before the thinning air would cause them difficulties. At least, the air *should* still be breathable, but.
. .

Strange violet lights began to flash soundlessly around his cockpit. He felt sure they were not in his head, nor were they ground bursts, unless the *Boches* had invented a long-range, silent explosive. There was no smell of smoke, just the usual odor of hot oil from the engine mingling with the freezing cold of high altitude in his nostrils.

Gradually the colorful display ceased to flash; the whole mass of cloud was suffused with eerie, roiling violet shapes. Max had never seen such remarkable atmospheric phenomena. But for the moment it did not appear threatening; a far more immediate problem was the relative proximity of the SPAD's service ceiling.

Abruptly he was jerked from his daydream. Emerging from the cloud into daylight, instead of what should have been an unbroken layer of cumulus below him the shocked pilot saw ground. Ground colored green; green fields, leafy green trees not the endless brown mud and shattered trunks of the war zone, but nevertheless ground - solid ground. And unaccountably he was barely fifteen meters above it.

Explanations must wait. Emergency. But before he could even drag back the stick a tall tree stretched out a limb, ripping a canvas panel from the lower wing. The SPAD shuddered and banked; he needed to correct the yaw with the joystick. If he was to land safely it must be at once.

He saw a grassy meadow. His veteran pilot's instincts took over. Dropping the wheels on to the bumpy field he brought the stricken aircraft down. Immediately the tail skid touched, he taxied into the cover of a hazel copse where the aircraft could be concealed, and cut the engine.

...

What sort of phenomenon could have given him the impression of climbing when he must have been diving? After more than twelve months in the

37

Aéronautique Militaire and five victories in dog fights, Max was still alive because he did not make rookie mistakes, not even in bad visibility. He took a deep breath, resting his forehead on the cockpit's leather-padded edge. No sound of guns. He was well behind the lines.

But whose lines?

Stripping off his sheepskin-lined flying jacket, a give-away of his identity, he climbed down from the cockpit clad only in shirt, breeches and brown leather knee boots, with his white silk scarf still knotted around his neck and kid flying gloves still on his hands.

Dappled sunlight filtered through the canopy above him; leaf litter crackled beneath his feet as he walked. He smelled the musk of fox, the damp mushroomy smell of rotting wood, natural scents gradually replacing the acrid, artificial fumes of aviation spirit in his nostrils.

Emerging into the open from the shade of the wood, he saw a gate in the boundary hedgerow. He began to make his way towards it, a little unsteady on his feet after so long in the air. He would have to risk being out in the open briefly, but as soon as possible he must conceal himself until he found out where he was.

His hopes of remaining undetected were instantly dashed. Before he even reached the hedge a stocky, long-haired man dressed in a frock coat and breeches appeared behind the gate and stared towards him. Max froze. Did Germans wear such odd clothes when out in the countryside? The man looked too big and strong for him to be able to chase after and subdue, especially in his present half-dazed state.

"Are you all right, friend? What a strange roll of thunder that was just now! I thought we were in for a storm."

Max sighed with relief. The man was speaking French. No doubt he had mistaken the rumble of the SPAD's engine for an augury of bad weather. The trees would have screened the low flying aircraft itself from his view.

"I thought so too. I took cover in the wood," Max called back.

"You took an awful risk!" exclaimed the traveler.

"From lightning you mean?"

"Not at all. From the Duke's foresters. They hang poachers, you know."

"What?" Max was baffled. "What Duke?"

"Orleans. The King's brother."

"I knew he was a bastard," Max shook his head. It was a simple fact not a moral judgment. "I didn't know he'd taken to hanging people without trial."

"Trial? What difference would a trial make for the likes of us? You're not from around here, are you?"

"Er. . . no. But I've studied law."

"Aha," the man nodded sagely. "I noticed the short hair. Where's your wig, eh? You've come for the big meeting in Arras."

"Arras? I. . ." Max had heard of no meeting. The French people were too caught up in common hatred of the external foe to devote much thought to the class enemies in their own government.

Nevertheless the man's error gave Max an excuse for being in a part of the countryside he didn't know. "Yes, that's right," he said.

"You look like a man of means. Very nice boots those, beautiful scarf. But you've got dirt on your face in the wood, did you know? And you should have brought an overcoat. It's a long walk, and the weather's going to turn cold."

"It was fine when I set out," said Max.

"You can't fool me," the man said, tapping the side of his nose. "No wig? No coat? I expect there were royalist troops out trying to intercept delegates. You hid the evidence somewhere. Everyone knows a lawyer by his wig and coat. But we're going to need lawyers. The *aristos* won't browbeat men like you, I'm thinking."

"They haven't managed it so far."

"Good man! You know, I can still hardly believe it - the first Estates General for over a century. Are you perhaps thinking of standing for election?"

"Election. . . " Max was still puzzled. There'd been no Estates General called in France since the brief assembly of 1789, over a century ago. That had led to a short-lived and violently suppressed insurrection. Ever since then French monarchs had ruled despotically; any popular movements that began to look promising had been outlawed, their leaders imprisoned until the populace could be distracted by the next convenient hostilities.

"Ah, perhaps. I haven't decided," he said.

"You should; you should. Louis XVI is not his father *The Well Beloved.* He's neglected his people long enough. Crushing taxes just to support that bloated court in opulence whilst honest poor people starve? We need lawyers - good talkers - the sort of men who'll persuade him of proper priorities, eh?"

"Louis XVI? . . . the king?" Max was taken aback.

"Most likely not his fault, I agree." The man interrupted quickly, as if worried that he had spoken too freely to a stranger. "Bad advisers to be sure."

"You think so?"

"Absolutely. But involving the people is the politics of the future, you mark my words. Just look how democracy is developing in the old British colonies in America. They'll build a great country there one day, you'll see."

"Ah, very probably, *Monsieur.. .?*"

"My name's Danton. Call me Georges."

Max stopped and stared at the man. With a great effort he gathered his distracted wits. He had just crash landed a SPAD. He knew that for a fact. Now here was a man talking about the era of Louis XVI, claiming to be the great Danton? Most likely an escaped lunatic. And yet he wore such strange clothes and he knew such historical details.

If only it were possible, what an opportunity such a thing would be! With the benefit of hindsight he could head off Mirabeau's treachery, save Danton from the guillotine, liberate the oppressed peasants from their chains. France could be a democracy, like the United States, like Britain. If Max could have his dearest wish, it would be to turn back time and throw in his lot with the man who should have been first president of a French Republic.

This was fantasy; reality was set in stone. But yet? Had he not just climbed for thirty minutes only to emerge above the cloud at a height of fifteen meters? Had he not just witnessed the most incredible light show in the skies? Who was he to be so certain of what was impossible?

If this was real, then the 1789 rising had not yet failed. Danton was alive. The man who might still be France's first president stood before him. All those fanciful dreams were within reach. Dare he even think of it? Was it conceivable he could change history, preventing a century of war? Had France by some miracle been given a second chance?

"You'd best come along with me," said Danton. "We'll be safer on the road together."

Max shook his head in wonder. "*Guide moi. Je te suis,*" he replied, smiling broadly, extending his hand. "Lead on. I'll follow you. I'm Max—Maximilien de Robespierre."

About the Author

Born in Yorkshire, Oxford graduate Philip Brian Hall is a former diplomat, teacher, and web designer. He has stood for parliament, sung solo in amateur operettas, rowed at Henley, and ridden in over one hundred steeplechases.

Philip's short stories, written mainly in speculative genres, have been published by *AE, The Canadian Science Fiction Review, T Gene Davis's Speculative Blog, The Sockdolager,* and The Flame Tree Publishing anthology, *Chilling Ghost Short Stories.* His first novel, *The Prophets of Baal,* is available in paperback and as an e-book.

He lives on a wee farm in Scotland with his wife, a dog, a cat, and some horses.

*****~~~~*****

Spirit Cat

by Hunter Liguore

With a dab of burnt sienna and a thin-tipped brush, the artist applied his name to the canvas. In recent years he shortened his first name to *J—J, no period, Willowby.* He hoped no one in the media would notice. J and Jay weren't much different, after all. If he were trying to be completely anonymous he would've signed an imposter's name. But they would never see the painting in America, not all the way from Cambodia. So, the artist kept his name. The name was all he had left.

The canvas was still wet, as J set it on the easel. He applied more strands of emerald green to fill out the foliage, the vast jungle that circled him, the canopy of broad-shaped leaves and bamboo clusters. The light was something he tried not to consider capturing accurately, since the sun moved overhead and shed strange shadows through the trees and large palm leaves throughout the day. It was his prerogative as the artist to leave things out.

J lit a cigarette and stretched, deliberating whether or not the piece was done. He wasn't one of those artists who couldn't commit to a finished work, endlessly adding layers and layers of imagination and paint. But he tried to get it right the first time—once was usually all he had to capture his subjects. He called to the spirit-cat lurking beneath a fig tree, sprawling, paws forward on the orchid-covered ground where wasps were plenty. If someone was watching him—tourists, fans, or Paparazzi—they would think he was talking to himself. The canvas was the only proof that something was hidden in the wood, and that too was questionable, J thought. Who would believe him?

But this was J Willowby, the same Jay Willowby who took the early twenty-first century art scene by storm with his anomalies, his portraits of the dead appearing to him. First it was nobodies, then it was the famous, until he had people lining up at his door to see if he could capture their deceased love ones partaking in the mysteries beyond the veil.

He didn't ask for the *gift*. When J thinks of his first spirit portrait, he thinks of starvation, of frozen bones and missing toes. It was the blizzard of 2022, when Cambridge turned to a city of glass, covered from wire to brick to mortar with ice. Harvard Park became an ice rink for the wealthy. He was one of the street tenants who sold his paintings to tourists in the square, but during the storm, he had nowhere to take shelter. His friends—*what friends*—turned a blind eye. Soup kitchens were packed, the churches filled, or he'd have to attend regular mass in exchange for a meal. He tried abandoned buildings, or under bridges, but frostbite set in; he hungered to the point that his stomach shriveled to the size of a walnut. When he collapsed, he remembered thinking he lived his life the way he wanted, an artist with no fame, but an artist true to his vision, his art and voice.

J had carried his portfolio with him at all times, tried to sell what he could to local businesses. When he felt the street freezing to his face, he thought someone might rob him for it, use it to build a fire. It was his only real possession, except for a beat-up watch, the kind you can get for two-dollars in a gumball machine, his father's army jacket, and a picture of his high school sweetheart, torn from *The Bostonian* when she married his best friend.

When J woke, he was lying in a hospital bed, warm, as if a stick of dynamite had been stuffed between his appendages. He was surprised that besides the routine visits from nurses and doctors, he also had visits from several locals, people he'd worked the circuit with, street performers, deacons, activists, some he hadn't seen in nearly a season.

Spirit Cat

When J was released from the hospital, he was discharged to a room at the YMCA, paid up by a patron for one month. His paints hardened, like globs of candy, which he soaked in water to resuscitate, and with the little art paper he had, he began painting portraits of those who had visited him in the hospital. It wasn't until he painted a portrait of a man named Asia, who used to work at the hospital, that he realized his subjects were dead. *Did you know, Asia? You've captured his essence perfectly. We really miss him.*

When spring arrived and J returned to the streets to sell his work, he was greeted by strangers awed at the coincidence that he had somehow painted their deceased friends and family. He had no explanation. Worked silently, figuring they'd all go away. Word spread. He was forced to vacate Harvard Square for a less palpable street corner near an organic beer garden. Not long afterwards, J was stopped by a famous face—Clint Eastwood. He thought nothing of it when Mr. Eastwood asked him to paint his portrait, though J noticed Eastwood didn't have that shriveled, dried-fruit, still-life face anymore. Last J had seen of him was on a TV through a window in a bar, a few years back, when Eastwood had been on the local news talking about his latest directorial effort. Eastwood had said one thing to J. "Don't make me look 103. Make me more like seventy." J painted the man he saw, full of spirit, with shadows and hard edges around his jaw, and eyes that gleamed with a well-lived look. *When I die, I want to have eyes like that,* thought J.

His Eastwood after-life fetched half a million dollars. J put it in the bank and continued working the streets, although he upgraded his art supplies and purchased a cell phone so he could call for take-out, rather than pack up his work in order to eat. Friday was his charity day. All of the money from the portraits he sold went to fund the soup kitchen. *My luck could change at any minute. They'll remember me, when I need them.*

But his luck continued. People from all walks of life, deceased with their living counterparts, flocked to him to get an after-life portrait done. J moved his work to the park by the statues of the Revolutionary War monument. Even there the crowds became too much, and he was asked by the authorities, and then the mayor, to get a shop.

His successes weren't the same ones the media reported in the paper. J fell in love countless times with young girls that met their death during the 2030s killing spree—he was also arrested as a suspect, having depicted the victims so candidly, and was later released when the real killer had been captured. J made love to the inconsolable, those who couldn't move past their own loss, and he looked into each of his lovers' eyes and said with a tone of finality, "Don't come to me when you cross over." Street artists painted his face in alleyways, on garbage dumpsters, and street signs. Art galleries begged for his work. He had speaking appearances, book deals, fan mail, and people who considered him a friend, though they'd never met him.

The highlight of his career, around his fortieth birthday, was supposed to be, according to *Life Magazine*, the day the President called him to paint a portrait of the family dog that died of old age. "We would be honored if you could paint Mr. Ted," said the President. But J didn't see the spirit dog, no matter how many days he spent at the White House as a guest. It had never happened to him before. He confided in the President's First Man, claiming that he didn't think he could do it, perhaps because it was an animal. No one would fault him, he thought. But when the President himself learned of the news, J was slightly discouraged. "Try," was all the President said.

Meanwhile, J started seeing the headlines, the lead stories, about his failure. To save face, J painted the dog from a photograph left in a drawer in the room he stayed in. Who would know he wasn't seeing the real spirit? He blended the colors of white and gray, which so often typified his work. When the President, First Man, and children, for which it was a gift, were presented with the painting, they were none the wiser. They loved it. The tabloids filled with pictures of the loving family with their after-life painting. The bad press was forgotten, forgiven. J never smiled during the affair and many days following, knowing he sold his soul for the ruse.

J traveled afterwards. Keeping a low profile, painting the spirits that did come to him. Sometimes he left the finished paintings on the front stoop for a family that suffered a recent loss. He didn't need the money, or the recognition. To absolve himself from committing fraud in his own work, he gave it away, seeing only the joy he believed it brought them. The Paparazzi started to follow him. Setup a hotline for people to call if they saw him, or better, received a painting. The reality Internet show, *Following in the Steps of Jay Willowby,* started as an indy project by one of his recipients, and was picked up the next season by the Network.

J dyed his hair, changed his look, and adapted a new style. He was no longer the loner dude with a baggy coat and mussed hair and beard. He went straight laced, hanging out in hotel bars, not seedy joints where a man would never be killed, but places people thought as much would happen by the look of it. He took lovers and left them before he could be found out, caught. He'd change his spots of habit. And after what seemed like endless years of running and disappearing, he stopped painting—that was the only thing that put an end to it. No painting. No need to see what Jay Willowby was up to.

He was fifty on the day the San Francisco Golden Gate Bridge collapsed in 2056. Close to 800 people perished. He had been living on a farm in East Hampton, Massachusetts, at the time, nearly three years without painting so much as a fingernail with colored marker. But the summons came the day the bridge fell. California wanted J to fly out to paint after-lifes of the deceased. Several mediums offered their services, if J would come, providing families with messages as well as portraits.

J waited to see if another painter with his talents would rise up, but none did. No fake ones either. He felt settled, despite an affair with the neighbor's wife, and a bastard child, which her husband wasn't any wiser about. She honored him by calling the girl, Jaycee. J thought he could make a go of this illusion, the tempered life of a man hitting midlife. Yet the dead still talked to him. They asked him to paint their essence. But he refused them, and he refused San Francisco.

Dreams started to take hold of his life, strange shapes and vivid horrors. Each week J awoke with a different terror. They were ghosts, not of people, but animals, ones he'd never seen before. The dreams kept him up at night. He started to sleep during the day. When this affected his work on the farm, he started to drink at night to dull the dreams, the hauntings.

In the fall of 2059 J woke from a demented dream, in which he was chased in his old neighborhood by a demon cat with the skin of a snake. No booze or pills made the cat go away. He started to lose his graying hair more rapidly. His belly fattened quicker than the sheep. Soon the neighbor's wife replaced him with a younger model. J knew what the cat wanted. Somehow, without a common language, it had told him to paint. But J couldn't, wasn't ready for the spotlight. He saw the headline in his head, *Reclusive Jay Willowby returns from the dead.*

J started to wake from his sleep, physically tormented by the snake-cat, covered in scars that looked like he'd considered suicide. His landlords, a simple couple, told him to seek help. J tried to hide the scars with bandages. When he sought refills for his sleeping pills, the prescribing doctor, upon seeing the gashes, had him committed to a 72-hour watch. During the night, in utter solitude and soberness, J talked to the cat. He was already in a mental hospital. What more could they do?

When he was released, J bought a one-way ticket to Cambodia. He followed the shadows, the cat's essence, through the airport, to the burgeoning town of Siem Reap, down winding paths, and into the hills, then the mountains, through ancient ruins, and back down in nameless towns, and through the jungle.

J set up his easel next to a small cave, where a mauled carcass, with the same leopard and snake-like swirl, mingled in the mud and dirt. He knew with surety that this was the remains of the spirit cat. He also sensed her unease over the encroaching humans. *Last. Last. Last.* That is what he heard from the cat. There were no more like it. Hunted and poached to extinction.

When J set the easel up, the marbled cat went and hid under the bushes. *Shy,* he thought with a smile, a first in so long. He remembered the countless dead he painted, and most were not shy. Only the cat. *Shy and unused to humans.* His paintbrushes were well preserved, considering all the years he left them unused. He purchased new paints for the trip, but hung onto a few of his old standbys that came to life when he soaked them in water. He worked a combination of acrylic and water, and brought in the colors of the foliage, which were locked in the ether where he saw the cat. *So unlike humans, who are shrouded in dark shadows.*

J spoke to the cat throughout his work. He talked about his life, what parts he remembered, like the time he painted for eighteen-hours to capture a young girl and her mother before they moved out of reach. They crossed over once they accepted death. *It's only another doorway,* J thought. Once they'd accept their fate, the light around the essence would flutter with diamonds, then fade. He worked fast. He had only one chance, a brief moment to capture them.

The more J painted, capturing the pointed ears that bowed out like two horns, or the long silky tail, or the stoic stance, the more he noticed a change in the cat's persona, its essence. The colors that surrounded it brightened even more. It turned jovial, playful, and dropped its guard. "You only want to be remembered," J told the cat.

When the painting was finished, J was surprised to see the marble cat still there. J lingered, smoking, breathing in the mildewed air, waiting, listening, then studying his finished work. What more could be done to capture the cat? What more could be done to settle its spirit? *That is my true art, to put the dead to rest.*

J called to the cat, friendly-like. Never having a pet his entire life, he cooed as if it was a baby, and called it *Marble* with endearment. He announced he was going for a walk to the cave. The cat followed.

J brought with him a shovel and set upon the task of burying the cat's carcass. He couldn't help himself from touching the fur, to feel just for a moment what the real thing might've felt like. *Which is your true essence?* he wondered. He covered the hole and placed a pretty orchid over the spot, along with a dribble of the local beer, which he drank heartily to quench his thirst. *You're free, now, my friend.*

J Willowby returned to the canvas. He studied his work, pleased it turned out so well; satisfied, he successfully captured the cat's spirit. *People will remember the marble cat; now, even future generations will know you, thanks to my work.* For a sudden moment, J thought he felt the absence of the cat, that it had moved on, now that he was packing up, the easel was away, the paint brushes cleaned. But in the dirt, rolling on its back, was Marble. *Time to go now, cat.*

That night J slept with ease knowing the cat would not haunt him. He drank moderately, no longer feeling he had to induce a state of coma in order to sleep. From his room, in a floating house on the ocean, J listened to the waves, until he fell fast asleep.

In the morning he awoke, his two legs stiff and unable to move. J thought at first he was stung by something poisonous, a spider perhaps, having read an article in the newspaper about such things happening. But when he investigated, he saw the marble cat sleeping sound, curled up in the crook of his legs. He moved her slowly, remembering the gashes. She stirred with a purr from his touch. *You have to go, now, friend, go to the after-life.*

J showered and went to town, where he sold the painting for a small pittance. The dealer knew the cat right away, having heard the news story about the cat being hunted to extinction. When asked how he was able to capture the cat's likeness, J didn't answer, only shrugged, and went on his way.

That night when he returned to his room, the marble cat was still there, this time waiting in a sitting position, more like a house cat, than a wild one. J set to work laying out his brushes and paints on the bed. The cat watched, poking the brushes with its spirit paw, or biting them with its teeth. J painted a second canvas of the cat through the night, falling fast asleep in the chair overlooking the water.

A burnt orange sun flooded the horizon with the stretching of dawn. The smell of fish took over the wind. J scribed his name to the painting, sure the cat would leave now—surely, two paintings would do it, but it stayed through the day, until the next morning, and even after the next painting.

By the end of the month J Willowby became known locally as the man who painted the marble cat. Twenty paintings in all comprised the collection and exhibit at the museum in Siem Reap. When his patrons asked him where he got his talent, J smiled and said it was as if the cat was with him, no longer extinct, but going along with him for the ride. "And if this were true, I might add," he told them, "I'd say the cat enjoys having her picture painted."

As the paintings sold one by one, discussions about the marble cat ensued. There was talk on the extensive mining and deforestation; people sought solutions. They looked to J for answers, but he simply told them he was only an artist. When J returned to his room he told the cat that people were fighting for her, and for others like her. He could tell this pleased Marble, but still she didn't leave.

People had started recognizing him as the Cat Man. J feared the phenomena that devoured his earlier life, and considered returning to America. *What would he do there that he couldn't do in Cambodia?* J sat with the cat in his lap. He'd grown attached to Marble and knew he couldn't ask her to leave her homeland. Instead, J packed his supplies and set off the following morning toward the next village.

When J arrived, he set up his easel. He watched the marble cat climb a fence and sit perched against the glow of a full moon and blue dusky sky. He painted her exotic likeness, each time seeing something he didn't see before, a new pattern in the fur, a different stance.

He did this in many villages throughout Cambodia. Word spread that the Cat Man had been there. People wondered who exactly this J Willowby was. His name faded and was replaced with simply, *Cat Man*. He didn't mind. No one hunted him, no one pushed him to extinction.

Years later, when travelers in the hills of the Cardamom Mountains found the artist's body, he had but one picture in his portfolio. The picture was a self-portrait with a marble cat held in one arm, surrounded by a myriad of color and light.

###

About the Author

Hunter Liguore is an American writer with degrees in history and writing. Her work has appeared in *Strange Horizons, Irish Times, New Plains Review, Writer's Chronicle, The Writer, Perihelion SF,* and an upcoming wildlife anthology from Ashland Creek Press. She is the first place recipient of the 2015 Ethnographic Fiction competition sponsored by the American Anthropological Association. She teaches undergraduate and graduate writing in New England. Her forthcoming novel, *Next Breath*, is represented by Regal Hoffman & Associates in New York.

*****〜〜〜〜〜*****

Ice-Cold

by Nyki Blatchley

Hugging the overcoat around me and ducking my head against the swirls of snow, I fought off the absurd idea I wanted an ice-cold beer. Why, for heaven's sake? Even if it weren't more the weather for steaming cocoa, I like beer coming out of the pump at a decent temperature, not half frozen.

It must be all those ads on telly. It seemed lately, whenever I switched the set on, some beer was being advertised, and, regardless of the brand, it was always "ice-cold." Good grief, was I really that susceptible to suggestion?

I wasn't the only one who'd noticed, but most people just grumbled that the advertisements were inappropriate in this weather. Then again, maybe they were automatically programmed according to the time of year. It was June, after all.

The wind's icy sharpness sliced down the street at me, flinging snow at my face, as I pushed through the pub door and slammed it gratefully behind me. Suddenly, gloriously warm, I stamped and shook the snow off me before moving off the mat.

Claire waved to me from the bar, and my heart lurched in pleasure, as usual. That is, it wasn't really my heart that lurched, but I wasn't complaining. Life was always exciting when Claire was around, and I could see from the eager gleam of her vivid green eyes that today was going to be no exception.

She kissed me with the enthusiasm she showed for everything and asked what I wanted to drink. Consciously resisting the urge to ask for an ice-cold beer, I got a pint of adequate ale instead and followed Claire to a table in an alcove.

"I've had a tip-off from one of my contacts," she said when we were shielded from the rest of the pub. "I think this is a big one, Steve."

I'd never been sure about Claire's contacts, who seemed to have information about everything from political corruption to the future plots of soap operas. She presented herself as an undercover activist—I wasn't even sure whether Claire was her real name, though I was pretty sure de Lune wasn't—but I sometimes wondered whether it was really all in her head. I didn't care, though: the excitement in those green eyes was worth a little self-deception.

I leant across the table to catch what she said better, and she mirrored the movement, bringing our faces only a couple of inches apart. "It's about the weather," she breathed. "It isn't natural."

"Huh?" I waited an instant, but she didn't add to the statement. "Well, of course it's not normal for it to be snowing in June, especially when the rest of the country's having a heat-wave."

"I said *natural*, not normal," she snapped, though her enthusiasm didn't leave room for true anger. "As in, someone's manipulating it."

I didn't answer. In normal circumstances, I'd have filed "manipulating the weather" alongside "abducted by aliens" and "Elvis working at the chip-shop," but this wasn't normal. The forecasters spouted on as expected about fronts and depressions, but it was easy to see they were panicking. Blizzards in June were bad enough, but when they were confined to a single city, the most bizarre explanations seemed plausible.

"Steve?" she demanded.

Realising I'd let the silence drag on, I nodded slowly, hoping that would show approval without committing myself to belief. "Do you know who?"

Claire grinned. "No, but my contact thought he knew where it was being done from. Feel like a bit of breaking and entering tonight?"

I was about to make an excuse, really I was, but I met those sparkling eyes again and found I'd already said yes.

...

"So, remind me again," I whispered, "why exactly we're breaking into a dry-cleaner's shop."

"It's a *front*, sweetheart." Claire had all the gear: black combat-style clothes, a black balaclava, and a sat-nav she consulted every few seconds, as if our location might have mysteriously changed. "These places are always a front for secret organisations: everyone knows that."

I examined the interior, trying to shield the flashlight so that no light leaked out of the front window, but it looked pretty regulation to me. I'd gone with dark, loose-fitting clothes, but I felt very unprepared beside Claire.

"So, how do we. . . ?"

She looked around with a hint of uncertainty, then shrugged. "Through the back, I suppose. Let's go and see."

The back room had dirty clothes hanging on one set of racks and clean clothes on another. I'd no idea what I was supposed to be looking for, and doubted there was anything to find, so it made me jump when I leant against the back wall and a panel swooshed open.

"You've found it," exclaimed Claire. "You're brilliant, Steve." She grabbed me and gave me a long, slow kiss that left me wondering whether there were any more hidden doors I could find.

Claire insisted on leading the way down, and I let her. It wasn't that I was scared, of course, but by her own account—and who was I to doubt that?—she had far more experience at this kind of thing. It was logical.

The stairs were utterly dark and seemed to go down forever. I kept close behind Claire, who gave off a beautiful scent of jasmine and excitement, until she paused at the bottom and eased another door open.

Light blinded me, and I squeezed my eyes shut. There was an indrawn breath, and Claire exclaimed, "Steve, you've got to look at this."

Squinting open one eye experimentally, I found the brightness tolerable and opened the other. Nevertheless, it was a few moments before I could make sense of anything.

The light from beyond the door came from televisions: ranks and files of them filling a vast space, all switched on. I could see no sign of anyone besides ourselves.

We wandered around, examining the televisions. As far as I could see, every one was showing the same thing: fur-clad men trudging relentlessly through a wilderness of snow and ice, drawing sleds behind them. I tried to remember tonight's schedules, but I couldn't recall anything like this, although I doubted I remembered more than a fraction of the channels available.

"This is familiar," murmured Claire. "I'd swear I've never seen it, but. . . "

I knew exactly what she meant. It was like a half-remembered dream, whose memory feels as real as any experience. It eluded every attempt to grasp it, so I levered my mind away from the problem.

"What's the point of all this?" I asked. "I mean, this is supposed to be where they're controlling the weather from, isn't it?" I couldn't believe I was taking that almost seriously. "What's this got to do with it? And why is no one here?"

"I don't think they come here much. My contact had to wait days to follow someone here. Perhaps they think a lot of coming and going would draw attention to this place. As to what it's got to do with the weather. . . "

She examined the nearest screen. "Well, the subject's appropriate, isn't it?"

"Yes, but—"

"Anyway, let's see if the sets are linked up to anything."

Linked up to what? Still, this whole thing was Claire's idea, so I investigated the leads emerging from the back of the nearest television. Besides the power cable, plugged into a socket on the floor, two lines led in opposite directions. I followed one, and Claire went the other way from a nearby set.

The lead I followed gradually joined others, bundled together and then the bundles bundled in their turn. At last, on the far side of the room, the whole collection vanished into a junction box, from which a single, slender connection was linked up to a DVD player.

I shook my head hard. Seriously? All these televisions were playing the same DVD? Whoever set it up had even left the case lying on top of the machine. *Scott of the Antarctic.*

"Steve?" Claire appeared around a row of televisions, her usually animated face looking stunned. "You'll never guess what I've found." She paused, exactly the right amount of time for dramatic effect. "Every one of the sets is *broadcasting.*"

"What? Where? Why? How?" I cursed myself silently. Couldn't I manage anything but journalistic interrogatives?

"And who," she added. "I don't really know, but I imagine they need all of these to produce a huge signal. That's why we recognised this. . . whatever it is."

"*Scott of the Antarctic,*" I put in, absurdly pleased at knowing something she didn't.

"Yes, that." She gave the cover a casual glance. "It's been bleeding over into the regular transmissions. It's a—another layer behind everything we've been watching. You know, subliminal."

59

"But why?"

Claire looked along the line of televisions. She glanced at me for a moment, then away again. "Steve," she said, her voice a little unsteady, "suppose. . . suppose that all this—not just these sets, but every single television in the city showing the same images—well, if all of this is blasting out into the air, maybe it could. . . affect the weather."

"Affect the weather? But how? Why? And who's doing it?" No, I obviously couldn't manage anything else.

"I've no idea who." She chewed her lower lip. "How? I don't know, but that broadcasting equipment looked like nothing I've ever seen before. But I imagine it's for money. Get the whole city in the grip of this sort of weather, then demand a huge amount of money to stop doing it."

"And you think anyone would believe them?" Strangely, that seemed the most implausible part of the whole theory.

She grinned. "I don't have to. It's whether *they* think anyone would believe them that's relevant."

I looked at the DVD cover. "So, you're saying that we're having blizzards in June, because every television's playing *Scott of the Antarctic*? In that case, all we have to do is turn it off."

Claire chewed her lip. "Not sure it's that simple."

"Why not?"

"Well, if this set-up has been controlling the weather all this time, just stopping that control dead might have terrible consequences."

I didn't really see why, but she could be right. "We could change the disk, couldn't we? Put on something that would reverse the effect." The flaw in my plan occurred to me. "At least, we could if we had another DVD."

Claire looked around. "There might be others here. Let's try there," she suggested, pointing at a metal cupboard on the nearest wall.

It was locked, but she had it open in seconds with what looked like a hairclip—she didn't use them in her hair, but she doubtless carried them for this purpose—to reveal an impressive DVD collection. I couldn't prevent myself from instinctively giving a quick scan for an adult section, but every title was connected in some way with climate or temperature. Clearly, winter wasn't the only effect they contemplated.

"This one'll do," she said. Stopping the machine, she changed the disc, putting *Scott of the Antarctic* carefully back in its case, set the permanent repeat, and pressed play. "Now, I think we're finished here. Let's go."

...

"Well, it's obviously still playing," said Claire, stretching out on my bed. Her sheen of sweat looked delicious, although I only felt enervated and uncomfortable.

"Seems like it," I said, opening a can. "Either they haven't noticed, or they haven't been back."

"Never mind, they'll check it out sooner or later and get picked up."

According to Claire, one of her contacts had a contact whose friend had a lover in MI5, and she'd passed word along to them. A few days ago, I might have doubted that, but Claire's contacts were clearly more genuine than I'd given her credit for.

Till this was cleared up, and the government scientists had been able to move in and shut the equipment down safely, the heat wave would continue. I couldn't complain, of course, considering that Claire had stripped down to her underwear to lie on my bed. Maybe it would get just a little hotter.

Still, I wouldn't be sorry when we got back to the good old four-seasons-in-an-hour climate we usually endured. In retrospect, perhaps we should have chosen

It's Come to Our Attention

footage of a balmy spring afternoon, rather than *The Towering Inferno.*

Picking up the can, I took a gulp of ice-cold beer.

About the Author

Nyki Blatchley graduated from Keele University in English and Greek and now lives just outside London, where he works as a freelance copywriter. He's had about forty stories published in publications such as *Penumbra, Lore, Wily Writers,* and *The Thirteenth Fontana Book of Great Horror Stories,* and his novel, *At An Uncertain Hour,* was released by StoneGarden in 2009.

*****~~~~*****

Chocolat

by James Dorr

"Bah! Chocolat!" It was even chocolate. Maurice threw down his newspaper in disgust.

Was nothing sacred?

The headline loomed up at him from the floor: *DEFINITION OF CHOCOLATE CHANGED.* It was in the newspaper's business section. An industry move to follow the lead of American food processors, to abolish the requirement that so much cocoa butter be contained to call a thing *chocolate*, had been passed by the European Union's Finance Council.

Finance indeed!

Maurice quivered with disgust. He, a *pensionnaire*, a veteran of two wars for the glory of France—and now it had come to this. Chirac had been bad enough, and then that, that *newcomer*, openly in the pocket of *le Président Americain.* Even this "socialist" now was no better. Acquiescing, even *leading* this latest attack against the very food the French people ate.

"You are what you eat," the thought came to him. An expression no doubt originally coined in France. And now, you eat chocolate, and you will be what? Up to 50 to 60 percent nothing more than cheap vegetable oil, so the article claimed!

He would have shivered, had it not been for the heat. Another "gift" of *l'industrie financière*, the ever-escalating summer warmth. People had died the last several years, those too poor to go to the mountains or to the coast for the August *vacances.*

But at least the French ate well, or so they once *had.* It had been France's legacy. Scientific papers had been written about Frenchmen's enviable long lives and excellent health.

Until now—

There had been riots the previous summer. Farmers on strike, blocking roads with their tractors, protesting the adulteration of produce. Of filling markets with cheap foreign imports. Until the <u>gendarmerie</u> came with water cannons.

You bought strawberries now, huge, plump, deep red—and tasting like paper! If you could even find real cream to put on them.

And beef, from England. In last week's news, a recent shipment suspected to have been infected by *la vache fou*—the "Disease of the Mad Cow."

Maurice felt himself melting.

We *ought* to object, he thought. The mayor, at least, should know. We, whose wellness, whose being, whose *substance* is put at risk by these— these businessmen!

Food made from chemicals. Hybridizations. Irradiated by who knows what?

If one could find fresh cream for one's paper strawberries, what kinds of poisons would *that* cow have eaten?

He felt his anger rise, boiling above his head. He pushed his front door open and oozed down the steps, into the street to join his fellow townspeople. Chanting with them: *Le maire! Le maire! Aussi la mairesse!*

Where were France's guillotines now, when they were needed?

Up to 50 to 60 percent cheap vegetable oil, indeed!

Maurice flowed with the crowd.

###

About the Author

Indiana writer James Dorr's *The Tears of Isis* was a 2014 Bram Stoker Award nominee for Superior Achievement in a Fiction Collection. Other books include *Strange Mistresses: Tales of Wonder and Romance, Darker Loves: Tales of Mystery and Regret,* and his all-poetry *Vamps (A Retrospective).* He's an Active Member of The Horror Writers Association and Science Fiction & Fantasy Writers of America, with nearly 400 individual appearances from *Alfred Hitchcock's Mystery Magazine* to *Xenophilia.* Dorr invites readers to visit his blog at http://jamesdorrwriter.wordpress.com.

*****~~~~~*****

The Thing Is, the Basement

by Greg Beatty

"But Father, I don't want to!"

"Chris. Everyone in this family has their own job to do, and getting things out of the basement is yours."

"I know that," I said, already getting my shoes out of the closet. But it didn't used to be my *only* job.

I took a long time lacing up my shoes, making sure I tucked the folded ends of the laces under. I tried those Velcro shoes once, thinking that they'd make it faster to get in and out of the basement, but then I stepped out of them once and lost them on the steps, and that's just too much of an adrenaline rush for me.

"Chris."

"I'm going, I'm going. Just let me get my flashlight."

Dad didn't protest. He knows that, depending on the basement, sometimes there's no light. I got the big MagnaFlash from the hall, the one that's bigger than the little bats they give out at bat day, and headed down the basement steps.

The steps were there. The light worked. I went downstairs. I got some canned goods, including some wax beans, and I came back upstairs.

"How was it?" Dad asked.

"There were stairs this time. I got some wax beans."

"Hey! Maybe I'm getting better," he said.

"Maybe." I set the beans on the counter for Mom.

I knew he wanted me to reassure him. I also knew that he was right: we all have our jobs to do, and reassuring him wasn't one of mine. Reassuring Dad was Mom's job, along with cooking, and charming the

67

neighbors who were allowed to visit on the ground floor and higher. Dad's jobs were to earn money, to praise Mom for how sexy she was when he thought I wasn't listening, and to build funky inventions.

Dad's attempt to combine two of his jobs was what had led to our current situation, and what had transformed my jobs from something pretty casual that, I admit, I complained about, into something I never complained about. I still complained about drying the dishes and taking out the trash, but I think that was more like an attempt to keep things normal, like calling Dad "Father" the way they did in old TV shows. It didn't work. When I complained, they let me stop doing the trash, and even stop drying the dishes, just so I still got things from the basement.

Things weren't normal. Things were so not normal that I sometimes wondered how the other kids at school couldn't tell. That's what I dreamt about, when I dreamed. That I'd go to school, and everybody could tell.

The teachers know something's up. They keep asking if my parents are fighting, and if there is some illness in my family that might be contributing to the way my grades have dropped from "their previous levels of achievement."

The counselors worry too. The last time I went in to talk about course selections, there were a bunch of pamphlets sitting out on the desk about anorexia. I'm not anorexic. I didn't want to lose the weight I lost. And it looks worse than it is. Some of it is just a growth spurt.

But I lost some of the weight because, sometimes, the basement makes me sick, you know? In the daytime, I'll be walking down the hall, headed for Algebra II class, just bopping with my friends, and I'll see Donna Weingarten wearing a blue sweater with a snag on one shoulder, and I'll think, "Oh, she got the dust off that sweater when they got it out of storage, it looks much better on her than I would have thought." And then I'll think how I shouldn't know that. I shouldn't know that sort of thing about Donna's winter clothes, unless she showed me herself.

And I might only feel a little sick, then, and it'll almost pass, and then I'll go to lunch, and I'll see Tim Bailey scooping the last of a little container of strawberry freezer jam, and complaining about how his mom's bitching at him for eating the rest of the jam, which she'd told him was being saved for a special event, and he hadn't eaten it, and when that happens, I'll finger the bruise on my knee, and I won't want to eat for a while.

Because I'll have eaten that freezer jam the night before. Dad will have sent me down into the basement, a basement, rather, and one where the steps don't quite fit. I'll have jumped down, and landed wrong, so that I smacked my leg on a couch, because other people's basements are never arranged like ours. They put their stuff in different places, and that's when I get banged up.

And after I spend so much effort getting down into that basement, and make so much noise that I scare myself, because I always think someone might hear me in their basement, and even though Dad's controls on the machine have only failed a couple of times, my heart is just pounding away like a mother, I feel like I deserve something for making it down into another basement. And so I pop open the Baileys's freezer, and I jam as many Dove bars and containers of freezer jam into my pockets and sometimes inside my clothes—I always wear baggy stuff these days, just in case—and then I try to make it back up the stairs. If there are any stairs. Except that sometimes I have to eat some of it right there, like a reward. I remember the way the edge of the plastic lid broke when I opened it, because it wasn't thawed, and how I had to lick and lick the frozen jam to really get the strawberry taste.

That was kind of cool, because I knew I wasn't supposed to lick it. I even licked one and put it back to freeze. But when Tim was hungry and complaining, even if he'd never starve and his mom still gave him the last of the jam, I felt like shit. I didn't eat that day.

And it's not like it's just food, or clothing, or just anything. It never stops. Every day I see something that I'm not supposed to know, and it ruins things for me. Like the collage that came in second in the ninth grade art show? As soon as they saw it, everyone else was saying how cool it was, and how it should have won. My first thoughts were, "Oh, so that was Helen in that picture? I wonder why she didn't use the one with her and the old grandpa looking guy?" And I can't ask, you know? And I can't see the collage, or the sweater, or the freezer jam, or the stained clothing, or anything, the same way as other people. I always know too much, too fast. From their basements.

Sometimes I wish I had more control over the basements. I mean, if it's going to happen, I wish I knew what kind of basement I was going to find, or at least whose. I know Dad has some sort of calibration device. I mean, in the beginning, it was all local, because we live in a planned community, and he had access to the exact dimensions of other local basements. Not just the dimensions, but the locations. Our suburb was supposed to be extra safe, since every place was already registered on GPS, and homeowners had the option of setting up little homing devices, so the kids could always "follow the chirp" to get home from wherever they were in the development. I still remember playing that game.

And for the first other basement, my dad didn't even tell me. He just stood near the steps looking like he was waiting for a package. Then I went down the steps, and everything was different, and Dad stood at the top of the stairs and laughed.

So, the first basement was nearby, and the fit was perfect. I didn't even stub my toe. It was still weird, of course. I was still where I wasn't supposed to be, but it was better, because it was close enough that I could pretend.

Then Dad started seeing how far he could go, and that really fucked things up. My ankle still tweaks me sometimes, from the first time he swapped a distant basement. There wasn't any place for the stairs to fit together, and there was so much stuff that nothing was on the shelves anymore. It all fell in a big heap. Some stuff was even pushed through other stuff, so that everywhere I looked there were all these weird things that never really existed. I saw something I called an Easy Bake Drill Press. The oven light still turned on, but all the cake pans had holes in them.

The folks who lived there used to have fish, too. I don't know if any of them lived. The lucky ones were just flopping, well, not on the floor, but on top of this moist, uneven pile of stuff, wriggling accidentally down in between cushions and souvenirs. The unlucky ones were shoved into other things. I tried to pull some of the wiggling tails out of the wall, before I realized they were stuck there. One tail came off in my hand. I didn't know what to do, so I put it in my pocket.

Dad and I had a big fight when I came back upstairs that night, except that we had to keep it really quiet, because Mom was talking to some people from the PTA in the living room.

She was hosting them. Dad and I were sort of hissing at each other, and that was the one time I asked him why, why he made me go down in the basement. Mom never did ask why. "For better or for worse," she always says. She was just mad, because I got sent into a basement while she had people over. Mom's that way.

For better or for worse. You know what was worse? Worse was the time Dad sent me into a basement, and it was full of pictures. That sounds better than it is. Everybody's got pictures, and if they don't have 'em in their basement, they've got 'em in their attic. This person, I

71

hope it was just one person, because if a family lived there—anyway, this person had pictures. At first I thought maybe they were all of his family, and he just had a lot of daughters and girl cousins, but there were too many of them, and they were all the same age. They were all young. They were all stuck to the wall, with lots of pins.

I think what made that basement worse was that it wasn't a foreign one. It was exactly the same as ours, and I went down the steps without noticing. I even took my hand off the banister. Until I saw all the stabbed girl pictures.

But you know what's worst of all? Dad can't get our basement back.

Doesn't that sound weirder than shit? He can keep changing basements, but he already knows his calibration's off. In fact, one time he said something that made me think that trying to put our basement back the way it originally was is how I ended up with a fish tail in my pocket. We can go into all the other basements we want to. We just can't get our own basement back.

At first, I didn't care. Going into the other basements, I was too young at first to realize it was wrong, and by the time I understood, I was used to it. I was good at it.

But then I'd see a box of Christmas lights on a shelf and I'd think, huh, it's been two full winters since we've hung our decorations. The first year, I think Mom was embarrassed that the front of our house was so bare, so last year, Dad bought an entire matching set of perfectly new lights. People admired our house. I missed the old decorations. Our decorations.

We used to have a pool table. Sometimes I wonder what happened to it. The felt must be really scratched up now. I mean, it isn't their pool table. I bet the sticks are broken and the balls chipped, even if it's just by accident, because they aren't used to it.

The Thing Is, the Basement

But you know what's worst of all? I go to school every day, and I know that someone else has been in my basement the night before, and I don't know it. And no one else in the whole school seems upset, and that—that's just not right. And then I think that it must be me. Either swapping basements is normal, and I just don't get it, or it's like a skill, and everyone else is just better at navigating strange basements. Or maybe something's the matter with me. That's the one I think at night.

But I know people should be upset. Sometimes I try to talk to Dad about it. "Father," I'll say, "The thing is, the basement. . . " and then my voice trails off, and I don't get any further.

And pretty soon, it's time to go downstairs again. And I always go.

###

About the Author

Since attending Clarion West in the summer of 2000, Greg Beatty has had stories published by *3SF, Abyss & Apex, Andromeda Spaceways Inflight Magazine, Fortean Bureau, HP Lovecraft's Magazine of Horror, Ideomancer, Oceans of the Mind, Paradox, SCI FICTION, Shadowed Realms,* and a number of other publications. He's also won a few flash fiction contests and writes nonfiction related to genre fiction, and poetry. His genre-related nonfiction has appeared in *Strange Horizons, The New York Review of Science Fiction*, and the *Internet Review of Science Fiction,* among other places. His poems have appeared in *Astropoetica, Absolute Magnitude, Abyss & Apex, Asimov's, Strange Horizons Star*Line,* and other venues, and one poem won the 2005 Rhysling Award in the short poem category.

*****~~~~*****

The Wishing Well

by Terri Bruce

The well lies in the center of town, granite stoned and moss covered. It has been there "forever," its provenance lost to history, and everyone around these parts knows it well. Picturesque and quaint, it sits on a well-trimmed swath of emerald-colored grass at the heart of the town green. It once served as a watering hole for farmers driving their sheep to the hundred acres of common pasture at the town's center, but that was long ago. Now it's known as the "wishing well," and many legends attach to it, though most seem to be yarns spun over the years by locals with quick wits and too little to keep them occupied: suicides and murders and, of course, hauntings. No one pays such stories any mind, and the few who seek to research these tales never turn up any historical evidence to support them. The well's supposed magical properties—health, fertility, long life, and good fortune—are similarly vague, yet generally accepted. Scientifically speaking, though, the most that can be proved is that the biocidal properties of the silver and copper coins tossed into it have kept the well's waters sweet and pure over the centuries, staving off cholera and typhoid epidemics that other villages were not so lucky to avoid.

The well is kept in good repair and is something of a local attraction. It is protected by a peaked roof, resting on white-painted supports, added in the 1950s by a local benefactor—some say in memorial to his young daughter who drowned in the well, but in reality as part of a spate of patriotic revival of civic duty that flared throughout the region and which also led to the erection of the bandstand

and the flagpole. The roof and supports are painted yearly, thanks to funds collected by the Rotarians. And though it is generally thought of as neat and tidy and traditional as any wishing well could want to be, visitors who come from all around to photograph it find the circle of drab gray stones small and unprepossessing, and they invariably go away slightly disappointed.

On May Day, a pole is erected on the green, and it is customary for all the unwed girls to toss a penny into the well for luck in love during the coming year, though there is more eye rolling now at this tradition than there was in years past. On Founders' Day, people of all ages troop to the well between bouts of burgers, ice cream, and water balloons to throw in a coin—usually a nickel or a dime—and make a wish, all in good fun, of course. It's the secret, solitary wishes, made under cover of dark by those creeping through the ankle-deep layer of fire-colored leaves crunching under foot or the ice-crusted snows of the winter's heart that are in earnest. *Please don't let it be cancer. Please make my husband stop drinking. Please don't let me lose the baby this time.* Even now when such things as wishes are out of fashion, people still come to the well and silently cast their coins in.

Those who find themselves passing by the well as they travel back roads on their way to somewhere else are usually drawn to stop and toss in a penny, almost as a reflexive response to some long-seated collective understanding that wells like this one—solitary and ancient—should not be passed by without their due. They were, after all, erected for a purpose, even if that purpose has long since been forgotten. And who knows—maybe magic wishing wells really do exist. Why not give it a try?

Most who come to the well find it impossible to simply toss their coin and leave, however. Instead, there's a compunction to stay and listen for the sound of their offering plunking through the water's surface and sinking into the dark, fathomless depths. There's a kind of pause or hush that opens in the world as the coin leaves the hand and arcs through the air. Hope? Reverence? Or perhaps it's unease.

A careful observer might note that all the wish makers stand far back from the well's edge, and even the rambunctious, noisy children who, on a dare from their peers, occasionally climb the supports to sit on the well's peaked roof are careful never to let a stray leg dangle above the well's black depths for more than a moment.

Those persons brave enough to lean on the cold, hard stones of the well's edge, worn smooth as eggs by time, and look in at the darkness of the still waters in an attempt to follow their coin's path as it sinks down to the bottom of the well see only the surface reflecting the racing clouds above like a mirror and revealing nothing of what might lie below. Standing this close, the cool, wet smell of dirt and stone tickles the nose, calling to mind the hushed depths of old-growth forests in late spring, when they are resplendent with still-furled ferns and new lichen and the smell of a recently fallen sprinkle of rain.

Far beneath the surface of the water, if one could see that far, down, down, down—far deeper than the usual few meters of a traditional hand-dug well—the well widens, becoming more of a cistern. Continuing further down, it widens again to become almost a cavern, and here, at the very bottom of the well, where the water is suffocatingly dark and deep with only the thinnest shaft of light to see by and no sound but the muffled weight of water, lies the accumulated wealth of ages, in copper and silver coins, layer upon layer thick. How deep do the coins lie? A foot? Five? Twenty-five? How many wishes have accumulated here? How many supplicants have come to this well, in jest and in earnest? It's hard to say.

While one might note the odd item here and there that has made its way to the bottom of the well over the centuries—shoes thrown by pranksters or lost by a daring child climbing the well's roof, a few cameras and cell phones dropped by outstretched arms trying to photograph the well's interior, and, in one case, a flute tossed by a frustrated student—what most naturally draws the eye here—and barely visible through the water's darkness—is the sapling-thick stake of iron, several feet high, ancient and battered, driven fast into a granite boulder centered in the well's silty, coin-covered bottom.

Affixed to the top of this stake is a strong ring of iron as rusted and pitted as the stake to which it is attached. To this ring is fastened a half-yard length of well-rusted—though still solid—heavy chain, the links each hand hammered and hand forged with primitive but sound craftsmanship and fitted together with the same care and precision that fitted the hundreds—thousands?—of fist-sized rocks that line the well's walls. The chain lies ponderously on the ground, far too heavy to be moved easily or swayed by the eddies of the well's waters. When and if the chain does move, it drags deep furrows in the accumulated coins, scattering and spreading them like sands of a mandala, with the slow, laborious rasping of metal on metal and sending a ripple across the surface of the well's waters.

The far end of this ponderous, heavy chain is attached to a thick and sturdy cuff of iron, this rougher and more crude in construction than the chain but just as unbreakable. This cuff is passed round the limb—perhaps one might call it an ankle—of something lumpen and misshapen and the color of old rust. At first it might appear to be a well-rusted and decaying object, massive and huge—a pile of fifty-gallon drums of toxic waste, an old Volkswagen Beetle, or perhaps a tattered old couch, bloated with water, with the springs sprung free.

And then it moves.

What first appeared to be leaching waste or motor oil or maybe even algae turns out to be a soft, bubbling skin of slime and muck that sloughs off in a continuous cloudy stream of brownish-red filth, polluting the waters and darkening them to the sickening color of dried blood. Underneath, giving form and structure to this frothing, pustulant morass, are pitted and decayed bones, the skeleton of some long dead animal—perhaps a wolf, perhaps a goat, but monstrously huge and misshapen. There are too many legs—or perhaps they are arms—and too many jutting ribs. Something resembling a face— certainly eyes and a mouth and teeth—appears and disappears in various places, and it's hard to say if it has just one set of each or many.

The primordial scum of the creature's "skin" is in constant motion, sliding and oozing into place over the brittle bones. At first, it appears the pollution appears to be streaming off of the creature and into the water, as if the thing is falling apart, and at others, it appears the pollution is flowing to it, pulled from the water to enlarge and strengthen it.

The creature glowers and glares, its rolling, slime-filmed eyes piercing in their madness and rage each time they appear. It is easy to imagine that the creature is remembering a time when it walked free, remembering the juicy crunch of bone and sinew in its ravening mouths and the screams and cries that filled the air, the delightful way skin peeled from the meat in long, satisfying strips, and the delicious ripping sound of arms and legs coming free from a body wish-boned between two clawed limbs.

Rather than ravening and frothing, the creature stands immobile, up to the iron cuff around its ankle in the coins, glaring balefully while its scummy skin sloughs and bubbles and its face blinks in and out of existence, waiting with malevolence and patience for the day when it will be free again. Here, in the dark, silent depths, the very stones of the well itself vibrate with the creature's simmering rage and madness and what must surely be dreams of shattering the iron cuff around its limb and pulling free of the iron chain and then, slowly, ever so slowly, climbing the moss-slicked sides of the well, digging into the space between the carefully fitted rocks for handholds, pulling itself up through the dark, cool waters of the well, and emerging into the light to once more stride across the world.

The thin trickle of watered-down light that reaches to the bottom of the well falters as a shadow flits across— a coin slowly sinking through the depths—and the creature shudders. The lidless eyes roll with dread and hatred as the quarter floats leisurely closer. The creature twitches, trying to avoid the coin—but there is nowhere for it to go. The iron chain holds it fast. The abomination shudders as the coin lands on the churning, seeping mass that is its body and burns its way through the outer coating, momentarily interrupting the flow of scum leaching to and from it. And now the true power of the well is revealed, for the purifying properties of copper and silver safeguard against not just cholera, but many kinds of impurities, including those that comprise the creature; without the frothing, scummy mass of its outer shell, it would be nothing more than a collection of brittle, old bones. However, the battle to drain away and purify the animating offal is never-ending; the monster's pollution renews and redoubles like a cancer, feeding on itself and ever growing. An ever-increasing number of coins are needed just to weaken the creature enough to hold it.

There are those who mock the custom of tossing a coin into a wishing well as old-fashioned or just plain foolish, but luckily the townsfolk hold fast to their traditions, and the well is not forgotten. Collective memory also exerts its influence, and passersby will always be drawn to stop and toss in a coin, even if they don't quite know why. There is little fear that the coins upon which we all depend for our safety will stop coming.

And yet, the power of the well to hold the creature wanes. The silver diluting and purifying the creature's sloughing pollution lessens day by day as newer coins— every year made of a little more nickel and a little less silver—slowly bury their more potent predecessors. Ever more coins are needed to hold the creature, and yet, every coin added weakens the power of the well to hold it. So make your wish and toss your coin—after all, every coin counts—but be sure to stand well back from the edge of the well when you do.

About the Author

Terri Bruce has been making up stories for as long as she can remember. Like Anne Shirley, she prefers to make people cry rather than laugh, but is happy if she can do either. She is the author of the paranormal contemporary fantasy "Afterlife" series, which includes *Hereafter* and *Thereafter*, and various short stories, including "Welcome to OASIS" (*Dear Robot* anthology, Kelly Ann Jacobson, November 2015) and "The Lady and the Unicorn" (NH Pulp Fiction *Live Free or Dragons* anthology, Plaidswede Publishing, Fall 2016).

*****~~~~~*****

The Argentine Radio

by Joel Richards

It took some time for the Argentine radio to be recognized as a fad. It didn't have the look of something new, not-seen-before, like the hula hoops of six decades past or the Beanie Babies of the 90's. It wasn't something active, like a dance craze, where people had to think about it to learn it. It just happened. People began to see these azure- and white-striped radios everywhere. Other people were pulling them out of handbags, pockets like a smartphone. Or carrying them like an iPod with earbuds attached. Except it wasn't a phone, and it couldn't access a universe of tunes. You couldn't personalize it or its contents. It had no contents.

It was just a radio.

…

Miguel Harrison enjoyed looking at his radio. He didn't know why.

Not many people questioned the why of it, but Miguel did. He blogged about pop culture and had a large following, mainly because he didn't go on and on about popular manifestations, but wrote about their larger, metameaning. If there was one. And that was what he was considering now.

Miguel's home office overlooked San Francisco Bay. Right now this was a vista of motion—lots of sailboats, some of them running before the wind with their colorful spinnakers deployed. This might have been a distraction, an attractive one, but that wasn't happening now. Miguel's attention was fixed on the Argentine radio upright on his desk, and it wasn't even on.

What was the appeal here? Possibly a retro thing, evoking nostalgia for the early Walkman? But most of today's listeners were too young to have owned a Walkman or even know about it. Perhaps the fad resembled the recent return of massive and colorful earphones where earbuds would do. But many thought the sound of the big earphones superior, and no one considered the Argentine radio an audio improvement of any sort.

There it was: a 3x5 inch handheld, striped like the Argentine flag—or maybe a soccer jersey—a volume control knob at the center where a camera lens might be if this were a camera, the knob embossed with the image of an Argentine coin, and otherwise a few simple tuning controls and displays, all digital. Nothing remarkable. But yet the Cool Factor—unexplainable but apparently big, big, big.

Even—so it seemed—to Miguel's mother.

…

Leonor Harrison's kitchen table was a major focal point of his parents' home—a primo social gathering place and a site of excellent dining. Sunday evenings were family time. Miguel would be there with his current love interest if she were suitable, on his own when between girl friends or with one he deemed not up to his mother's scrutiny.

Leonor was a thoroughly modern Latina outwardly, yet with distinct, well-rooted core values. Eclectic tastes, too. She proved that to her parents by marrying Tom Harrison. She worked as a website designer in SoMa. This was Sunday, though, and her creative efforts were reserved for the kitchen. She could cook up a magnificent *porotos granados* or *pastel de choclo*, then talk over it at dinner about possible improvements to Miguel's home page. Or Miguel's girl friends or prospective ones.

The Argentine Radio

"I think the next one will be a Latina, eh Miguel?" The slight curl of a smile let Miguel know that this was a tease.

Tom Harrison looked on, with his own smile of amusement. He'd heard this dialogue before.

"Because Stacey was an Anglo, right?" Miguel answered back.

"Stacey was six months ago. And yes, you seem to alternate, go back and forth. Not that I disapprove, you know. Because I don't."

"I do know, Mama. But there's nothing happening in that department right now. It's work and more work."

As if in a reminder of this, Miguel's glance turned to the sideboard where the wine bottle for tonight's dinner stood—along with an Argentine radio.

"Mama," he said. "That radio."

"Yes?"

"It's Argentine. You're Chilean. Why not a Chilean radio?"

"Because there isn't one. If there is, find me one."

"I don't think you want a Chilean radio," Miguel's father said.

Leonor's cheeks colored.

"It's true. I like that radio. But it's just a blue-and-white radio that I like."

"I think it's a little more than that," Tom Harrison said.

"What can I say?" Leonor threw up her hands. "It's cute."

...

Miguel took that conversation home with him, along with the leftover *pastel*. He thought on the drive home about what had been said. He looked at the Argentine radio, still on his desk. He didn't find it cute, but he did find it compelling. He found even the thought of it compelling.

And why was that?

...

Miguel did his research on the company that made the radio. There was a manufacturing facility in an industrial park outside Buenos Aires. That seemed strange. Surely such a low-tech product could be assembled far more cheaply offshore—China, Taiwan, or wherever. The manufacturing facility likely wasn't the heart of the company. That turned out to be true. A call to the factory confirmed that its chief was not an officer of the company. He claimed to not interact much with corporate headquarters, whose address was that of a law firm in downtown Buenos Aires.

According to the public filings, the company's officers all bore the most common of names: chairman, Juan Perez; president and CEO, Joaquin Rodriguez; vice president, Roberto Garcia, and so on down the slate.

Miguel sent off an email, in Spanish, to Ronaldo Fernandez, the company's director of public relations, asking if the president would agree to an interview. He included his credits and past publications, dating back to print media. Within the hour he got back a response stating that the company and its principals, as a matter of policy, did not grant interviews.

...

Miguel dreamed that night. He had taken the radio to his night table and tuned it to the classical music station. By coincidence or happenstance—though Miguel no longer believed in coincidence or happenstance when it concerned the radio—the selection was by Astor Piazzolla. Miguel listened to the tango-inspired composition till he became drowsy, then turned off the radio and the light.

Time passed and dreams came. Miguel dreamed of a copper astrolabe whose image haunted a shah in its command of his every waking moment, till he ordered it sunk in the deepest sea. He dreamt of tigers, a parade of sinuosity and movement. He dreamed of an old blind man who could not see, yet anyone who saw him could not forget the image. He dreamt of an old coin, mysteriously inscribed and which itself inscribed its likeness on the cerebral cortex of whomever had held it.

Miguel awoke with complete memory of what he had dreamt and knowing what he had on his bedside table.

...

It was 6:30 in San Francisco, 10:30 in Buenos Aires. Miguel picked up the phone and called Ronaldo Fernandez. Somewhat surprisingly, his call was passed through.

Sr. Fernandez was agreeable but undisclosing, very much a director of public relations. He told Miguel that it was his function to field all inquiries. He and the company responded to all of them; they valued courtesy. However, the response to all inquiries was that the company and its principals did not discuss its products or its business strategies.

"Fair enough, Sr. Fernandez," Miguel said. "But would you ask your president whether he would discuss Jorge Luis Borges?"

There was a moment of silence, then a soft chuckle.

"I will indeed, Sr. Harrison. I have been waiting longer than I had expected for that question to be asked. Please give me again your contact information, your personal telephone number, preferably. Our president is in a meeting at the moment, but I believe I can promise you a call back within the hour."

...

Miguel welcomed the interval. He thought about the Zahir, that being or thing—of which there can only be one in the world at a time—that "possesses the terrible property of being unforgettable, and whose image finally drives one mad." His radio wasn't driving him mad, nor was he obsessed by it. He more than liked the radio—he had feelings for it. He certainly didn't want to rid himself of the Zahir, as had Borges. And it wasn't one of a kind. He clearly was not the possessor of the Zahir in its entirety. That certainly wouldn't have served the purposes of a marketing company seeking to sell its products in mass.

He had something that partook of the nature of the Zahir, but was somehow not quite it. How could that be?

It would take President Rodriguez to illuminate that.

...

"So nice to find someone in the journalism line with a taste for literature," Sr. Rodriguez said. The voice was different from the media relations director's, but the chuckle was not.

"Are you an admirer of Borges, Sr. Harrison?"

"I am," Miguel said. "Of course I have my favorites."

"As do we all. And what are yours?"

"First and foremost, 'The Zahir.' I find the story itself a variation of the Zahir. I think about it often, though not to the point of obsession."

"I would hope not," Sr. Rodriguez said. "A story is not a tangible that you could give or throw away."

"Not everyone wants to be rid of the Zahir," Miguel said. "But you seem to have created an aspect of the Zahir. . . and you are selling it."

"Yes." A silence followed.

Miguel spoke into it. "Would you be good enough to tell me how?"

"I will do so, Sr. Harrison. It was bound to come out, and we are actually embracing of this. We were simply searching for the right person, the best venue for doing so, and we seem to have found it in you."

"You left some direction. The Argentine colors, the coin-embossed tuning button."

The Argentine Radio

"Coins do indeed figure into it," Sr. Rodrigues said. "Not only in the Zahir of Borges' account. My father had a news kiosk at the Plaza San Martin. He knew Borges in his later days. Borges bought his newspaper from my father, even when his sight was almost gone. It was a daily ritual. I imagine he had someone at home to read it to him. Of course, my father had read 'The Zahir.' Perhaps he had even discussed the story with Borges. In any case, my father collected many of the coins that Borges gave him in payment, particularly any older, interesting ones. At his death he had a good-sized leather pouch with many of those coins. I inherited them."

Miguel felt the room closing in. There was room for only one thing in his sight, his inner sight, a vision of such a bag, its leather worn smooth from handling, its heft almost palpable.

"We took those coins and had them pulverized to the finest metallic powder, then further reduced to nanoparticle size. We can then mix them into polymers. The volume button of each of our radios has a trace of those coins in its composition. We wanted only a trace. We wanted to entrance our customers, not obsess them."

"And of course, that content in each radio is what makes it impossible to replicate by knock-off artists."

"That was our intent."

"You don't know which of those coins was the Zahir, then?" Miguel asked.

"No. Perhaps the totality of the coins was the Zahir."

Throughout, Miguel had been picking up on subvocalizations. He had been given a great story. And yet there was something more here. Even in his exultation, Miguel found himself alive to a tinge of wistfulness, deep attachment that had not been sundered or given away.

"Forgive me, Sr. Rodriguez. You have been so forthcoming, and I am grateful. May I ask you—and you need not answer—did you include all the coins in the moneybag in the manufacturing process?"

Yet another silence.

"You are very perceptive, young man. I held one coin back—chosen at random. I felt that it must be a random process. I shaved and ground a few millimeters from its circumference, and included that metal with the rest. I had to, of course. That coin, randomly selected or not—and perhaps it had selected me rather than I, it—could have been the Zahir. So even part of that had to be in the mix. But I could not bring myself to part with that last coin." He paused.

"I'm sure you can understand why."

###

About the Author

Joel Richards has done one novel, *Pindharee* (published by Tor), but is mainly a short fiction writer. He's appeared in a number of original anthologies, including Terry Carr's *Universe* series, Roger Zelazny's *Warriors of Blood and Dream,* Harry Turtledove's *Alternate Generals II,* and a broad range of magazines. In the last couple of years, he's had three novelettes/short stories in *Asimov's* and one in *Analog.*

*****~~~~~*****

All True

by Marie DesJardin

Alyssa knew she was going to be fired when Jeremy invited her to lunch. Jeremy always invited his staff to lunch when he fired them. He'd read that a positive environment helped to offset an unpleasant experience. He may have been right; Alyssa hadn't heard of anyone sounding particularly bitter afterwards—although, of course, they weren't around very long after the event to voice their complaints.

Alyssa didn't want to be fired. She loved being a Soup Taster. She cherished the fragrant bench where she dipped into various concoctions, inhaling the seductive vapors, cleansing her palate afterward with sorbet. She liked the company-supplied silver spoons that had "Guaranteed not to bend" stamped into the handle. None of hers had ever bent, either—not that she'd tried.

Jeremy took Alyssa to Paco's, the most exclusive Chinese restaurant in town. ("With a name like Paco's, it *has* to be good.") The maître d' gave them the table near the back. "The firing table," according to rumor. That clinched it; her head was on the block. Still, Alyssa knew she'd enjoy the restaurant; Paco's had a splendid way with spices.

On their way in, Alyssa passed a table where a skinny woman was devouring a bowl of fried ice cream. Either she had the metabolism of a gerbil, or that high-fat reducing diet Alyssa'd recently read about actually worked. The next table over sat another woman who could only be described as "plain." Despite this, she had three model-handsome men vying for her attention. The cover of the most recent *Woman's Adviser* magazine leapt to Alyssa's mind: *Ten ways for any woman to charm any man!* While Alyssa considered this a welcome change from the usual *Transform everything about your face, mind, and figure to attract the man of your dreams* hype, she believed it no more than the other approach. More likely, the plain woman was a director or producer, and the men were "talent" trying to impress her.

Jeremy pulled out Alyssa's chair. She thanked him and sat.

"And what would *Monsieur et Mademoiselle* like to drink?" asked their waiter, apparently unaware of the already dual ethnic nature of his establishment. Or perhaps he'd read in *Cultured Cuisine* that a French accent produces better tips. Alyssa had seen that article, too.

"Any wine with a favorable review would be fine with me," Jeremy answered, seating himself. "Alyssa?"

Alyssa waved a hand. "Whatever."

"*Immédiatement.*"

The man bowed and went, while a minion scurried up with a pitcher filled with chilled ice water and orange slices. Alyssa was intrigued; a recent study claimed that oranges actually improved the taste of the water an additional four percent over the traditional lemon slice. She sniffed, and then took an appraising sip from her newly filled crystal goblet. It *did* seem particularly refreshing; perhaps it was just the novelty.

Jeremy set aside his unread menu. "What would you like, Alyssa?"

"I hear the pork ribs here are fabulous."

Jeremy hesitated. "Beef is better for you. According to the USDA—"

Alyssa rolled her eyes. "Good grief, Jeremy, do you believe everything you read? This is Paco's. I want pork."

Jeremy frowned. "If the studies weren't reliable, they wouldn't publish them."

Alyssa was spared a response by the arrival of their bottle of white wine. Alyssa preferred red, but she remembered Jeremy's qualification about the good review, and the media *had* been touting the virtues of white lately. The waiter made the most of the ritual presentation, opening, and pouring of the wine. It sparkled invitingly. She swirled, sniffed, and took a conscious sip. Not bad. Just the right amount of citrus.

"Are you ready to order?" the man asked.

"Yes," Jeremy said decisively. "I'll have your special of the day. And the lady would like. . . pork ribs."

The waiter nodded solemnly.

Jeremy murmured to him, "I know that beef is better for you, but the lady—"

The waiter raised his hand. "I quite understand, *Monsieur*. We are happy to serve *Mademoiselle* whatever she prefers. Not everything must come with an endorsement."

"Thank you."

Alyssa gritted her teeth as the waiter walked away. What was wrong with simply ordering what you liked? Was everyone on the planet a sheep?

Annoyed, Alyssa looked away. She instantly regretted it, because the people at the next table were sloppily nibbling fried wontons. She looked again. The people were trying to eat fried wontons with a *spoon*. The four of them repeatedly strove to balance the rigid objects on their silverware, snapping at them hastily as the wontons fell back to the plate.

Alyssa stared. She'd read something about this. . . Oh, yes. A poster in the break room: *Ten Ways to Identify a Space Alien*. She'd forgotten the other signs, but she remembered the bit about them eating fried foods with a spoon. Maybe the author had eaten at this restaurant.

Jeremy cleared his throat. "Alyssa, you've been with us for some time—"

Ah. Here came the speech. "Two years."

"And you've performed admirably. You've helped make Tempted Tongue Soups the legend they are today."

Alyssa wasn't fooled. "But. . . "

"But, your error the other day. . . you know the one."

"Mistaking the rosemary for basil."

Jeremy shrugged helplessly. "We can't have it. Rosemary and basil are completely different herbs. Even a layman can tell the difference. To an educated palate like yours—"

"I had allergies that day—temporary allergies. They're over now."

"Allergies!" Jeremy sat up. "Had I known you harbored this defect—"

"It was *one day*. Some new flower blooming."

"Duration is no excuse. Do you think a murderer should walk free because he says to the judge, 'I'm sorry, Your Honor, but I only fired my gun into a crowded elevator *one day*?'"

A wonton clattered to the plate. Distracted, Alyssa couldn't help saying, "Did you notice that the people next to us are eating fried wontons with a spoon?"

"I never order an appetizer." Jeremy sniffed critically in their direction. "Cheese. Not very ethnic."

"It's using the spoon that's unusual." Alyssa covertly studied the foursome. "Maybe they're drama students, trying to get a reaction."

"Possibly. After all, their clothes match."

"Excuse me?"

"If they were wearing mismatched clothing while engaged in bizarre eating behaviors, I might suspect them to be space aliens. But this bunch seems fairly well-attired." Jeremy pondered. "I wonder how they'd react to my smartphone."

"What?"

"Exhibiting mood swings in the vicinity of advanced machinery would be another indication of space alien origin." He felt his pockets. "I must have left it in my coat."

Alyssa stared. "You're seriously considering the space alien idea?"

Jeremy looked up blandly. "The article describing the ten signs was quite specific."

"That was a *joke*."

"I don't understand how you can dismiss printed information out of hand. In all areas of specialized knowledge, experts define the critical criteria. If the criteria are met, the subject is in compliance. If the subject is *out* of compliance. For example, if the subject has a previously undisclosed personal failing, then that person might. . . get fired."

Alyssa slumped. "So, I'm fired."

Jeremy looked contrite. "We can't make exceptions."

"Because of one incident."

"My hands are tied."

"Whoever made up that rule didn't have allergies, did they?"

Jeremy smiled sadly. "I'm sorry. Drink your wine. It's living up to its recommendation, don't you think?"

Alyssa took another sip. It *was* rather good. Perhaps Jeremy was right about trusting the so-called experts. After all, here she was, drinking white wine between a quartet of suspected space aliens, the thinnest gorging woman on the planet, and a plain woman flirting with several fawning men, all while being fired from her beloved job. Life was strange.

Or perhaps it only *seemed* strange because Alyssa hadn't yet realized what everyone else had. What if she'd continually overlooked resources available to her, simply because as a sensible person she had never believed in them? For example, the ten ways to identify a space alien. Or how to charm any man or lose weight through eating ice cream.

Ages ago, Alyssa had received a junk email purporting that anyone could use "Amazing Mind

Command" to change their life. Women could command men to fall in love with them. People could command strangers to give them money on the street. And bosses could be commanded to give their employees a raise. Alyssa had always remembered that bit about the raise.

Alyssa returned her attention to Jeremy, who was idly observing their alien neighbors as they tried to drink their citrus water through straws stuck in their noses.

What if these wild assertions were true? What if no one had tried Amazing Mind Command, simply because their better sense told them not to? Alyssa was already fired. She had nothing to lose.

Determinedly, she focused her attention on Jeremy the way the brochure had described. She let her mind become still and clear, the way it was when she tasted a new soup. She set her doubts aside. As of this moment, the ways of the universe were open to her. The underlying reality was hers to command. Those really were space aliens at the neighboring table. Women did lose weight by eating ice cream. Every wine, food, and book ever favorably reviewed had merit. People daily fell in love with the oddest people and didn't know why.

You will keep me on staff, Alyssa mind-commanded Jeremy. *You realize that Tempted Tongue's success is due mainly to me. You would do anything other than let me go.*

Jeremy merely continued sipping, watching his neighbors with a rather vacant expression.

It was time to engage the aliens. *I know you can hear me*, Alyssa mind-commanded the extraterrestrials. *Use your telepathic powers to aid me. Aliens are always telepathic. Help me, and I will ease your path onto this planet.*

The quartet continued as before, but Alyssa noticed a difference in her partner. Jeremy drew back slightly. His gaze wandered over her shoulder.

Alyssa increased her concentration. *You will not fire me*, she commanded fiercely. *I am essential to your success.*

Jeremy became almost rigid. It was working!

She started as a voice, directly behind her, announced, "*Monsieur, Mademoiselle.* Your order."

Disoriented, Alyssa watched a young man place their dishes before them. The aroma of perfectly prepared pork tickled her nose, but Alyssa bitterly swallowed her chagrin. So much for mind control; Jeremy's altered behavior had been due to nothing more than his noticing their food approaching. She poked at her pork with a knife. Given her previous skepticism, it was amazing how disappointed she felt.

Jeremy dug into his dish with gusto. "So," he said around a mouthful, "We're agreed? The corner office?"

Alyssa looked up quickly. "What?"

Jeremy raised his glass. "We can't have our new Taste Director sitting in the common area, can we?"

Alyssa searched Jeremy's face. He seemed sincere. Dazedly, she said, "That would be fine."

"Wonderful. I can't wait to see what new taste temptations you come up with."

Alyssa quickly looked at the next table. The space aliens were setting dollar bills, one at a time, on top of the closed folder for their restaurant bill—which was floating about an inch above the tablecloth.

Jeremy gazed at her plate. "Could I try a piece of your pork?"

###

About the Author

Marie DesJardin's short fiction credits include *Analog Science Fiction and Fact, Apokrupha, Flash Fiction Online, Michael Moorcock's New Worlds*

Magazine, Star Quake 2, and *Story Quest.* She has one published science fiction novel and is developing a new series.

In her day job, she works for a video surveillance company, which means she never has to ask what anyone else is doing, because she already knows. She loves travel, animals, and hiking in the mountains when they are not on fire.

*****~~~~~*****

The Translator

by Arthur M. Doweyko

The cat spoke.

"Meow."

<I'm hungry>

Gerrard Plotkin adjusted his earphones. Fluffy sat by her empty food bowl and spoke again. "Meoww."

<I'm really hungry>

Gerrard jumped, sending her in a screech across the kitchen's linoleum floor.

"Sorry about that."

He poured some dry food into her bowl and sat back down at the table. His grin was almost painful. He reached out with a trembling finger and switched off The Translator. His science project, circuit boards threaded with frayed wiring and cabling, took up the length of the kitchen table. The Science Fair weekend loomed but a day off.

The mudroom's trapdoor jerked open, and Wolf loped in. The German Shepherd paused long enough to sniff the air.

"Woof."

<Happy to see you>

Gerrard couldn't believe his ears.

"Me, too."

The dog trotted over and nuzzled his leg. Gerrard reached up to a cabinet and pulled out a box of treats.

"Come on, boy. You like these. What do y'say?"

Wolf stood up on his hind legs.

"Come on, say something."

The dog whined and uttered a short yelp.

<Please give me >

99

Gerrard tossed his earphones on the table and ran out of the kitchen through the dining room, screaming. "It works! It works!" Wolf chased him into the living room. They turned up a corner of the hall rug and raced up the stairs to Gerrard's bedroom. Wolf slobbered over his buddy as they wrestled on his bed.

A few minutes later, Gerrard lay on the tussled bed covers. His arm caressed Wolf, who nestled his nose into an inviting armpit. He was still breathing heavily when the front door clicked open.

"Gerry. You here?"

It was his stepbrother, Brady, a sophomore at Hamden High. Saturday morning football practice was over.

"Hey, squirt. Are you upstairs?"

Gerrard ran to the top of the stairs with Wolf close at his heels. "Brady! It works! It works!"

Brady took a step into the kitchen and threw his gear into a corner. "You mean that pile of junk?" By the time Gerrard arrived, he was at the refrigerator gulping down an open milk container.

"That's not junk. You're looking at 'The Translator.'"

Brady kicked the fridge door closed. "And it's supposed to do what?"

"Watch. You'll see." Gerrard held up the ear phones. "Just listen."

Wolf sauntered into the kitchen. Gerrard grabbed the treats and held them over the dog's head. "Come on, boy. You want these, right?"

Brady asked, "What am I supposed to hear?"

"Just listen. Listen when Wolf says something."

After a few more jiggles of the box, Wolf spoke up.

"Woof."

Gerrard looked up at his brother. "Well?"

"I got nothing."

100

One of the earphone banana plugs lay on the table.

"Hold on. This thing got pulled out."

"Later, buddy. Gotta get washed up." Brady patted Gerrard on the head and darted up the stairs.

Gerrard donned the earphones. "Damn it, Brady. You always treat me like a kid. This thing really works. You'll see."

The voice from upstairs echoed from the bathroom. "Gerry, you're the smartest one in the family. You're gonna win the science fair for sure."

<Gerry, you're a geek and you got no chance at the science fair>

"What did you say?"

"You're a genius, Gerry."

<You're a nerd, Gerry>

Gerrard slumped into a kitchen chair. The Translator analyzed high frequency wave patterns associated with mammalian speech. Subtle tones related to emotion were correlated with intent and the programming converted the original sounds to speech.

He gazed at the pile on the table. He never thought about humans, the most devious of all the mammals. The Translator was more than an interpreter of animal speech—it was a lie detector. Even better, it turned the lie inside out. He rubbed the back of his neck, feeling the dampness that had settled there. The earphones slipped down as the front door swung open.

"Hi, Gerry. Is your brother home yet?" His stepmother, Trudie, nudged the door aside with her elbow and wiggled through with an armload of groceries.

"He's upstairs, washing up."

"Give your dad a hand, will you honey? What is all this?"

"Trudie, I told you last night. It's my science fair project. I was testing it out."

"Honey, I told you to use the workbench in the cellar. And please stop calling me Trudie."

"I was just getting it ready for this weekend. . . Mom."

"As soon as you bring in the groceries, I want you to clean up this mess."

Gerrard brought up his earphones. "This is important to me."

"Of course, dear."

<Annoying little child>

"Now, go help your dad."

<Stop bothering me>

Gerrard tossed the earphones and ran out the door.

"Hey Gerry, just in time." His father handed him two bags. "Everything all right, kiddo?"

Gerrard turned his face away to hide the moisture which ran across his cheek. "Sure, Dad. I'll be right back for the rest."

. . .

After supper, he sat on the edge of his bed and swung his legs over the carpet, sneaker toes arcing over the reassembled Translator. Fluffy's nose peeked from under the bed, while Wolf curled up next to him. He pushed back on his glasses. Nerd of the Year, that's what he was. The Translator was more than just a high school science project. It was a turning point—animals could talk, and even better, people couldn't lie. The world would be changed forever. Maybe he should get it patented. Maybe he'd get the Nobel Prize. And maybe he should keep it a secret.

"Jane is here, Gerry. Are you ready?"

Trudie's voice jerked him out of his funk. He was old enough to recognize self-pity, and it wasn't the first time. His new mom meant well, but would never fill the void. He pivoted off the bed and stuck his head out the door. "Hey, Jane, I'm up here. Can you come up here for a second before we go?"

Brady was at the base of the stairs. "Hurry up, Gerry, I don't got all night." It was Friday night at the movies, and his stepbrother's grumpy voice made it clear he was less than amused to be the chaperone.

Jane appeared at the doorway. "Hi, Ger. What's that?"

Six out of seven days, she was no more than the girl next door. A year ahead of him at school, she was the closest thing to a real friend he had.

"My project. I call it The Translator."

"What's it do?"

Gerrard donned the earphones and flicked a switch. "It's really cool. Let it warm up, and I'll show you."

Jane sat down next to him. His pulse raced. He wasn't sure if it was from the chance to show Jane The Translator at work, or from the smell of her perfume.

"Jane, it's just a test. So don't go all wonky when I ask you a question."

She nodded. His hands felt cold. He looked up at her and asked, "Ready?"

"Now!" Brady was at the door. "We're going to be late."

"Damn it, Brady."

Jane patted Gerrard on the shoulder and said, "There'll be another time, Ger."

"I guess."

…

The rules were strict. Live animals weren't allowed at the Annual Claphorn High School Science Fair. Judges from nearby colleges and industry waltzed through Gerrard's aisle in groups of two or three. He had set up his equipment on a folding table with a large poster showing a cat meowing and words coming out of the earphones. The lack of electrical outlets made the exhibit more show than tell. Although The Translator garnered some respectful nods, he caught a muffled snicker or two as the judges passed by. He knew deep inside that no one really believed the machine actually worked. Why would they?

The girl with a display next to his—the one which claimed that classical music made plants grow better—was getting way more attention, mostly because she was blonde, pretty, and had two potted plants to show.

A few minutes before closing time, Jane showed up. Her sandy hair looped up over her head, making her smile appear even wider. "Sorry I'm so late, Ger. How's it going?"

"The judges came through already. I don't think they believe the machine works."

"Then, they're not so smart." Jane moved closer. "I believe you."

"But you haven't tried it yet."

"I don't have to."

Gerrard braced himself against the display table as his legs melted. Sweat beaded at his temples. "Maybe when I get home, you could come by. I could show you."

Jane's mom waved from one of the exit doors.

"Oh, my ride's here. I can't make it tonight. Rain check?"

"For sure."

"I'll try and come over tomorrow night."

Jane skipped away. For a moment, the light from the front doors turned her dress translucent. She became an angel as she liquefied into the glare. A bell sounded. The Science Fair was over.

. . .

"You should've been there, Dad. There were so many people. And there were some really cool exhibits."

"I bet yours was one of the best. By the way, your mom and I feel awful, son, but we had to visit with the Daytons. . . you know. . . your mom's best friend just came back from the hospital."

"Yeah, I suppose. And she's not *my* mom."

"Now, now, Gerrard. She's doing the best she can."

"Whatever."

The Translator

His father looked down at the pile of wires and boxes. The lack of a judges' certificate turned his face down. "Son, don't feel bad about the Science Fair. I'm sure you'll knock their socks off next year."

…

Gerrard sauntered over to the refrigerator, snagged a soda can, and disappeared into the living room to watch TV with his father.

Trudie appeared at the kitchen door. "Aren't you going to tell him to move that junk down to the basement?"

"Give him a little space, dear. He worked hard on that project. I think he needs a little time to recover."

"If you ask me, that boy's got his head in the clouds."

Yesterday was gone, but Gerrard's head kept spinning as he watched a detective corner a suspect in a dark alley. The dick had his gun out and pushed the barrel into a beady-eyed suspect's mouth.

"You're gonna tell me all about it, Mooch ... all about Katie and how she fell from her apartment window." He flicked his head to the side. *"Your buddy there, he ain't in no shape to talk. . . but you still are. . . leastways, for now."*

Mooch mumbled.

The dick pulled back the revolver. "What's that? I can't hear you."

"I got nothin' to say. I can't help it if a dumb dame falls out a window, and besides, I wasn't even in town yesterday."

The two rolled to the ground. A muffled shot rang out.

"Son, did you finish your homework? Tomorrow's Monday."

"Right after this, dad. It's almost over."

If the detective had The Translator, he'd know right away what really happened. Gerrard pictured himself

105

on TV, on the news. *SIXTEEN-YEAR-OLD-BOY INVENTS THE ULTIMATE LIE DETECTOR.* He'd be famous. He'd change the world—no more lies, no more deception—besides, he'd be rich. *A sweet life.*

Later that night, Gerrard planned out his strategy.

...

"What's in the box, Mr. Plotkin?"

Mr. Angus Tracy was a stickler who had a fervent distaste for chaos. Science class was no place for creative diversions.

"Sir, I brought in my science project. I was hoping I could demonstrate it to the class."

Tracy's eyes rolled up. Gerrard suspected the man was getting senile, especially with his obsession with order—everything had its place. The man looked over the class as if gauging potential interest. "Remind us again, Mr. Plotkin, what your project is all about."

Gerrard stood up from his seat and swallowed. "I call it The Translator. I designed it to interpret the sounds animals make and generate an English language translation." He ignored the giggles from the rear of the classroom. "It's based on the wavelength and frequency of a sound correlated to emotion. I wrote an algorithm to substitute words for those sounds."

Tracy interrupted. "Mr. Plotkin, as you can see there are no animals here to demonstrate your. . . your invention."

"Oh, but there are, Mr. Tracy."

A brief blush passed over the teacher's face.

"I found that The Translator works with humans, too. But unlike dogs and cats, it changes what they say to what they really mean."

"*Really,* Mr. Plotkin. That hardly seems possible."

"It'll take just a minute to plug it in. I can show you."

The Translator

The gigglers in the rear piped up and seconded the suggestion. Others in the class joined in. Suddenly, everyone wanted to see The Translator at work.

Mr. Tracy cleared off a section of a counter. "Bring it here. I'll help you set it up."

Several minutes later, the countertop looked like Gerrard's kitchen table.

"Sir, can we use your amp there for the audio output?"

Tracy gave Gerrard a "what for?" look.

"So that everyone can hear the translation."

Gerrard fiddled with several switches. A low-pitched humming filled the room. "It's all set, sir." The twittering died down, and his classmates' smiles faded away. Maybe the machine worked. Who would want their words twisted to reveal their true meaning?

"Now, class, we need someone to volunteer, to say something aloud so that this. . . Mr. Plotkin's Translator can be tested."

<Don't volunteer. Just be quiet so you don't embarrass Mr. Plotkin>

The stilted, artificial speech hung in the air for a moment. Tracy whispered, "I don't think that was funny."

Gerrard flicked a switch, and the humming died off. "It was The Translator. I told you, it changes your words. . . into what you really mean."

"Nonsense. Make another joke, and you'll be explaining it to the headmaster." He turned back to the class. "I want a volunteer. . . now."

No one stirred.

"Very well, then, Mr. Jeffries, you've always got something to say. Why not stand up and give us a statement. Give Mr. Plotkin's machine here a real test."

Macy Jeffries was an ogre. His marginal wit and abundant weight over-qualified him for the position of class oaf. He was the last person Gerrard wanted to see standing.

107

Cajoled by his buddies, Macy wiggled out of his seat.

Tracy nodded to Gerrard. "Turn it on."

The hum beckoned to Macy.

"That crap machine of yours is a fake, and you're a bigger fake, Gerrardo."

<Take care. That machine can embarrass me, Gerrard>

Macy turned beet red. "I didn't say that, you little jerk."

<That's what I meant to say. You're no jerk>

"Mr. Tracy. . . the shrimp just dissed me. Are you gonna let him get away with it?"

Tracy's mouth twisted. He pulled out the amp plugs. "I don't know how you did that, Mr. Plotkin. You've embarrassed me as well as your classmates. Such behavior will not go unpunished."

"But, it wasn't me, Mr. Tracy. You heard it yourself. You—"

Led by Macy, the class broke into laughter. Mr. Tracy escorted Gerrard and his equipment into the hallway. "Stand out here, while I decide what to do with you."

…

The ride home was uneventful. His dad didn't speak until they pulled into the driveway. "It's late, but I think Mom's got your dinner in the fridge."

"Dad, I didn't do anything wrong. Everybody thinks I faked it all."

"I believe you, Gerry. Trouble is, nobody else does. Sometimes that's just the way it is, kiddo."

"It sucks."

His dad patted him on the head. "Now, go on up to your room. By the way, Jane came by the house before I left. She wanted to talk to you and might still be here."

Gerrard angled through the back door, arms wrapped about The Translator. Trudie shouted out from the kitchen. "Jane's upstairs. Don't dilly-dally. It's late, and she should be going home. Tell her you're about to have dinner, and you've got to get cleaned up. She'll understand."

Wolf leaped out of the bedroom doorway and knocked Gerrard back to the head of the stairs. "Whoah, boy. You almost killed me. Do we have a guest inside?"

Jane's smile felt like sunshine.

Gerrard kicked his box to the foot of the bed as she stood. "Ger, I heard what happened at school."

"Yeah, that. It wasn't my fault. Mr. Tracy—you know. . ."

"Ger, everyone at school was talking about it."

"So, what are they saying? I mean—"

"It doesn't matter what they're saying. I know you. And I know that you're honest and hard working. That Translator of yours has to be the real thing."

"Thanks, Jane. You're probably the only one that believes me, and you haven't even seen it work."

Trudie's voice echoed up along the stairway. "Gerrard. Dinner's ready. Have you washed up, yet?"

"Damn. Dinner."

"Sounds like I should leave now."

Gerrard walked Jane to the doorway. "Thanks for coming."

"Ger, how long does it take to fire up that thing?"

"A minute or so. You want to see it work *now*?"

"Yes, now."

Gerrard stepped to the head of the stairs. "Trudie. . . Mom, I'll be right down. Jane's leaving."

He ran back into the bedroom and pulled out several components from the box. After connecting a few wires, he threw on the earphones and plugged the power cord into the wall.

Jane asked, "Well?"

He sat on the floor tuning his invention. "Give it a second."

Jane reached down. "Is this the microphone?"

Gerrard nodded. "Hold on. I'll get Wolf."

Jane shook her head and said, "Ger, I love you."

Gerrard's heart caught in his throat. A second later, a mechanical voice erupted through his earphones, his eyes widened, and the stars danced across his bedroom ceiling.

About the Author

Arthur Doweyko has authored over 100 scientific papers, invented novel 3D drug design software, and shares the 2008 Thomas Alva Edison Patent Award for the discovery of Sprycel, a new anti-cancer drug. He writes science fiction and fantasy. His novels include *Algorithm* (2010 RPLA award), published in 2014, and *Angela's Apple* (Best Pre-Pub Sci-Fi RPLA 2014), under contract. He has published numerous award-winning short stories, teaches college chemistry, and wanders the beaches when not jousting with aliens.

*****~~~~~*****

Something in Forever

by E. M. Eastick

They float to earth as ash and settle on the flowers of Mother's blackberry bushes in the early morning light of July twelfth. The leaves, the grass, the thorns are untouched. The flowers curl in, as if retreating from poison, but three days later, plump purple fruit loads the branches, dragging them down almost flat with the earth.

I pluck a handful and regard the swollen berries, technically not a berry at all but an aggregate fruit, a product of not one but many female parts that grow and fuse. Mother doesn't know what an aggregate fruit is. She says it's no use learning anything that's no use for anything. That's probably why I don't attend school with the kids from town, but learn what I can from T.V. and the spattering of books my father brings home from goodness knows where, the tavern, I suppose.

The fruit brushes my lips with the purple stain I know it will leave. The juice oozes over my tongue and through the gaps in my teeth, the sweetness full and embracing with the promise of feeling content forever.

Mother buys three new buckets from Black's Hardware Store. She ducks her head and fluffs her graying hair when Jess asks how things are at home, and then promises a pie or two, if Jess is interested. Mother heads to Hill's for meat, perhaps minced pork or turkey thighs, while I linger at McGuire's. Through the glass I ogle the rainbow gobstoppers and twisty licorice, the rock candy and the caramel chews, and stuff my nose through the doorway when Pete Miller steps out of the shop, the open door releasing a waft of sugar smell and cinnamon. Old mean Mrs. McGuire shoos me away. She knows Mother won't stand for treats, even if we could afford them.

The buckets rattle in the back of the Chevy as we bump down the driveway and pull up by the side gate. Mother steps out, her khaki trousers flawless if not for a tiny tear at the left shin. I know she bears a matching scratch on her right hand from when she, too, couldn't resist scrambling through the brambles to sample the bumper crop. I guess the scratch will heal. I'm not so sure she'll mend the pants.

"Get pickin', Sal." Mother swings the buckets out of the back and into my arms. "There's twelve pies ordered already."

I get pickin'. The sun hovers overhead, as if to defy the passing of time, as if summer will last an eternity and the brambles will always be rich with fruit. I pick and pick and pick and pick. The juice stains my skin and mixes with pricks of blood. The earthy smell of sweet mingles with the acrid stench of a crushed beetle. When the first bucket brims with fruit and my arms are tired from picking, I crumble into the grass and lie on my back. The sky looms with iridescent blue, the sun blinding. I wish for clouds. I wish for noise. I wish for something to change, but Mother says it never will. Never is a long time, I tell her.

After three days of baking, the brambles still flourish. Mother buys two more buckets and ushers me into the yard earlier today than yesterday. "Make hay while the sun shines," she says through a swollen top lip, the smile grotesquely skewed and not my mother's at all.

I pick and pick and pick and pick. The spindly branches slap my shins and claw at my knees as I venture deeper into the bushes, determined to claim the ripest, fattest, juiciest fruit.

Mother rattles into town and sells the pies. I never see the money. I never see her smile, but the new secondhand runners fit well enough and offer toe room where the others didn't. I bounce into the yard and pick, proud to contribute, pleased with my new old shoes, hopeful of a coat before winter, a coat that doesn't pull under the arms and across my shoulders when I crouch to pat Rowdy.

#

Years later, Jess Black dies. So does grouchy old Mrs. McGuire, who passes the store to her twisty-faced son, Gerald. I thought he was my age, but he lived with his dad on the other side of town, and I rarely saw him anyway. Now he's old and fat and bald and sour. His teeth look brown and worn—probably from too much candy—when he offers a snarly smile as I eye the treats in the window on the way to Hill's to fetch ground beef.

Mother's surprised about Jess. "I went to school with her." She raises tentative fingers to her hair, still rich with auburn between the grey, and turns to the kitchen window. The reflection dulls the scar on her cheek and the ring of a bruise round her neck.

"Jess was old, Mom." I slip past her and open the fridge. The empty shelves mirror my empty stomach if not for the fill of blackberries that morning, and I flick the door closed and listen for the suck on the seal. It doesn't suck like it used to. I knew it wouldn't. Only new fridges suck.

To distract myself, I retreat to my bedroom with my father's latest tavern offering, a book about the universe, illustrated with balls of fire and globes of gas. My stagnant world spins with white dwarfs and supernovas and planetary nebula, until I become timeless, too, a speck of nothing in forever.

More old folks pass, as old folks do, but I never really notice the changing faces in town. I only notice the farm and how slowly Father tends to the animals. He hobbles to the barn to check Brandy, Bailey's only foal, already fifteen hands and as headstrong as any horse before her. Father returns to the house with Rowdy

113

plodding along beside him. Rowdy's muzzle is grey and low and uninterested in puppy smells.

The books stop coming when Father dies the next winter, not long after Rowdy. Within days, the bruises fade on Mother's face. She takes me to McGuire's candy store as a treat from the dead. I mourn the lack of reading material over peanut brittle and licorice. The light of the shop glows on Mother's cheeks and brightens her eyes to a startling blue I've never noticed before.

"Looks like we're in for a warm spring," says Gerald, and I wonder how he knows. I wonder if I'll ever get a new coat. Even when winters are mild, it's always cold to me. Mother smiles and nods as if to assure me my old coat works just fine.

"Yep, it's going to be a warm one." Gerard screws his face into what must be a smile, tight and lined with wrinkles, and hands me a rainbow gobstopper in an unusual display of benevolence.

The blackberries flourish. Mother bakes and sells the pies to new customers, the butcher's son, Harry, and Jess Black's granddaughter, Milly. The cow's stiff with milk, which we churn and freeze and add to our food, creamy asparagus and corn, buttery pork and chicken. Mother's trousers grow tight, and we trade pies and butter and cream for new clothes, even a new secondhand coat—at last. It's not much bigger than my old one, but the holes are fewer, and the extra length snuggles around my hips.

We sell the horses to Jo Kelly in exchange for a puppy, a border collie crossed with something rusty and wild, an accidental parent with dubious genes. I name her Tessa and take her with me to the blackberry bushes to chase the leafhoppers and tiny white butterflies that crowd the clover, but after the first prick, a tiny dot of blood rising on her nose, she skulks away and lies in the grass.

The pies sell to faces I barely recognize. Jess Black's granddaughter sells the hardware store, and marries an import, an outhouse-type man who fells timber along the Franklin. I see her with a baby, and then a toddler, and then two. The hardware store closes, tumbles, transforms into a stand of townhomes, sleek with steel and glassy eyes for windows.

Mother takes up pottery and spins cups and vases and odd-shaped things that she pretends are meant to lean that way. She asks me if I'd like to move on, sell the farm to greedy developers in exchange for a sleek new condo. There would be money enough to live comfortably, never worrying about dogs or horses or how full a cow's udders are.

"What about the blackberries?" Does she think I haven't noticed our agelessness, or that I never figured out why?

Her silence tells me she's thinking, wondering where to steer our lives. "The world's changing, Sal, but we're not."

"So?"

More silence tells me she's probing an argument, weighing its merits before she speaks. "We're cursed with deathlessness."

"We're blessed with immortality. Can't you see that?"

She closes her eyes against seeing. "I want to die someday, just like everyone else."

"I want to live, keep on living, like this forever." My book on the universe is weathered and worn, browning at the page edges and crumbling at the spine, but still it's my favorite of Father's gifts. It explains the miracle. It justifies my life.

And so it's decided. We'll keep the blackberries for me alone.

Mother shows me the loose stone by the fireplace, the tin box full of notes and coins, and explains their worth in the new world. She hands me a notebook of recipes compiled and perfected over masses of time and suggests a value for each formula if treated with love and respect and a touch of smarts. To make it easier for me, we lie in the grass by the blackberry bushes, an aging faithful Tessa beside us, and watch the clouds shift into new illusions.

"I was wrong," Mother says quietly. "Things *do* change. They *can* change, if you want them to. It's too late for me, but you. . ." She holds my hand and squeezes her love.

"You have time now, Mother," I plead. "All the time in the universe."

When I rise on my elbow and look at her face, her eyes are closed, her features serene. Not a strand of grey hair marks her head. Her skin is smooth and fresh, and the vision of her youth stabs me to the heart.

Through a blur of tears, I bury her there, by the blackberries, under a spindly branch heavy with fruit and speckled with a fresh dusting of ash. Night falls around me, and I lie in the grass watching the stars shift overhead. They are still and silent and tireless with eternal light. For a long time I stare at the stars and wonder which one is their home. Maybe someday, I'll get to visit them, too.

###

About the Author

E. M. Eastick is a retired environmental professional, born and raised in Australia and currently living in Colorado. Her creative efforts can be found in *The Literary Hatchet, Alimentum,* and *Mad Scientist Journal.*

*****~~~~*****

Deja Vu

by Lisa Timpf

A dank curtain of darkness had fallen by the time I left the office. The solar-powered streetlights barely pierced the murk, and the damp air left an unwholesome film against my cheek as I wended my way home through the almost-deserted streets.

It was the time of year I loathed with a vengeance—pitch black when I went to work, ditto at go-home time. It got harder and harder to take every year.

What made it worse was that there were sections of my commute that it wasn't strictly safe to traverse without adequate light. Fortunately, the atom torch's blue glow, combined with the hand laser I packed in a visible location, provided sufficient deterrent for any would-be assailants, who tended to prefer softer targets.

This used to be a good neighbourhood. I chewed on that thought as I walked, my spring-soled shoes rebounding lightly from the plastacrete surface. Since the Antibiotic Failure Plague, it seemed everything had gone you-know-where in a Hydrean hand basket, street safety included.

I shook my head. I've never been a starry-eyed optimist, but I'm not usually given to dwelling on the negative, either. *I need a distraction, a getaway, that's all,* I told myself. When I got home, I flipped on the TVcomp and punched a few ideas in the keypad as I absentmindedly sucked on a tube of protein ration.

Nowhere super hot, like Florida. Forget the tropics, you had to stay under a bubble there. I preferred fresh air. That narrowed the options.

117

Then I saw the specials for the 2072 Kentucky Derby. I never went to horse races. I hated crowds.

I also needed to shake myself out of my comfort zone. Besides, Kentucky was still a wide-open state, without the massive dun-colored plastadomes dotting the landscape in far too many places, ever since people got jumpy about the prospect of Plague contagion lingering in the air. All nonsense, of course, but the corporate interests who manufacture the 'domes and their workings have a vested interest in convincing people otherwise.

I made my booking before I could change my mind. Kentucky Derby it was.

...

The vibrancy of the horses as they pranced to the starting gate, the brilliance of the silks, the buzz of the crowd, the snapping of pennants in the wind—the whole spectacle made me feel more alive than I'd felt in months, years maybe. *This is just what I needed,* I told myself.

As I hunched over to study the program, deciding where to dedicate my slim allotment of betting money, I felt my eyebrows rise of their own accord when I read the name of DarbyKing's owner.

I pondered for a moment, tapping the program against my forehead. I don't usually believe in signs, but this one was flashing in hit-you-between-the-eyes neon. It was too significant to ignore.

I went to the auto teller and took out enough money to make me hyperventilate. Then I got in the lineup. I made it to the wicket just in time.

As I headed back to my seat, my forehead beaded with sweat, I wasn't certain that making it in time was a good thing.

The horses disappeared into the starting gate, and there was silence for a moment. My skin tingled in anticipation, and I wondered why I hadn't done this sort of thing before.

Deja Vu

I can't afford it, that's why, I told myself. *I must be crazy, betting that kind of money.*

Then the gates flew open.

The large view screen at the centre of the track's infield and the updates provided in the announcer's excited staccato helped me keep tabs on DarbyKing's progress. At the start, the big red horse was right up with the front-runners. It stayed that way right up to the homestretch.

I'm not usually one for displays of emotion. Doesn't matter. I found myself on my feet screaming along with the rest of the crowd as the horses pounded toward the finish line. DarbyKing was neck and neck with Silver Starburst, the hands-down favourite. Coming up quickly from behind was Call Me Courageous, a jet-black horse with a white blaze smack down the middle of his face.

They were two lengths away from the finish line, the three of them side by side, and if I thought the decibel level was insane before, it notched up to a whole new level. Just when it seemed that a photo finish was inevitable, DarbyKing pulled away ever so slightly, bunching his hindquarters and leaping across the finish line just ahead of his challengers.

I jumped up and down a couple more times, then stopped and stood still, letting it sink in.

My horse had won.

My horse had long odds.

That meant—well, that meant I had a pile of money coming to me.

I shuffled toward the wicket to pick up the cash, nursing an unwelcome, niggling thought that refused to go away.

There was something familiar in the horse's stride, as if I'd *seen* it before.

That doesn't make sense, I told myself. How would I recognize a racehorse when I didn't follow racing?

The niggling thought that I'd seen the animal before was still bothering me when I boarded the hoptrain back to the City.

I peered through the plastaglass. The fog had really settled in. It was like we were hopping through pea soup. White pea soup, minus the chunks of speed-raised cow-ham.

I thought back to the name of the DarbyKing's owner. Luke Jurgens.

It may not be the *same* Luke Jurgens, I reasoned with myself.

But it could be.

And I thought back to the day I met him. And that's when I remembered.

...

"I'm Luke," the tall, blonde-haired man sitting to my virtual left leaned over to introduce himself.

"Remi," I replied, extending my hand in turn. My virtual hand, that is. I was in the comfort of my study, participating in the class remotely, and Jurgens was—well, I don't know where he was, but I know where he wasn't, and that's in the class in person.

I'd taken Wykopf's advanced genetics class, because I was interested in the subject matter. Maybe that's only partly true. I took it to show off how smart I was. I thought I was smart in those days.

Anyway, I ended up next to Jurgens by chance that day, and although he bantered throughout the session, distracting me from Wykopf's teaching, I put up with it. In fact, I sat beside him for the rest of the semester. Why? Because Luke was handsome and funny. He had that charismatic streak that runs through certain people, that makes you feel illuminated and larger than life—that makes you feel as though anything could happen in their presence.

Deja Vu

Wykopf's cryptic style of lecturing left the bulk of the class hopelessly lost, but his explanations made *sense* to me, so I could afford to listen with a split focus.

Luke couldn't afford the split focus, but neither could he help bantering and goofing off. After the first week of virtual classes, Luke and I realized that we actually lived in the same town in *non*-virtual reality. In exchange for allowing me to bask in his presence, I helped Luke with his advanced genetics homework. We'd get together at his place, I'd explain the tricky parts, and then we'd go for a few ricebeers.

But back to why DarbyKing seemed familiar. Thinking about Luke must have made my memory cells root around in the rooms set aside for my university days, because they came up with the appropriate recollection. The clue was a vidclip, remastered from film, that Professor Natlack showed in the scantly-attended sport history class.

A vidclip of the legendary racehorse, Man O' War.

I pondered, staring out the window at the fog.

In the burning and looting that followed the Plague, a lot of historic records had been lost. Natlack's generation had been the last to really believe in the importance of the past; thanks to the pressures of advertising and media, it was all about having a good time in the present and looking forward to the promise of a better future.

Odds were, there were only a handful of people left who might recognize DarbyKing's resemblance to Man O' War.

Should I say something, or not?

I debated the merits of both ends of that question the rest of the way home.

...

I'd lost track of Luke, after university. It took awhile to track him down. It took awhile longer to convince him to meet at our old favourite dive bar.

We caught up on things over the first ricebeer. It's potent stuff, which is why it was our drink of choice back in university. After the second round arrived, I judged it safe to ask him why he did it.

"You figured it out, huh?" he commented. He leaned forward and continued in a whisper. "I did it, because Man O' War deserved a chance at the big race."

"What you did was *wrong*," I hissed. "You cheated a lot of people."

"They chose to bet, or not to bet, on a horse," he shrugged. "Not my fault."

"If they'd known who and what he was. . . " I let my voice trail off.

He turned to face me. "He won't race again. It was a one-shot deal."

"I can see where you wouldn't want to take the risk." I recognized the superiority in my tone and despised myself for it. "How much did you bet? A billion? A couple trillion?"

"I didn't bet anything," he said, a note of injury in his voice. "I wanted to see if he could really win the Derby."

I leaned back. What he said about not betting wouldn't be credible, if you were talking about the average person. Luke wasn't the average person. His dad had struck it rich in the colony-outfitting business. He really didn't need the money.

"How. . . " I was curious in spite of myself.

"I used Thorrburn's Theory, about cellular-level memory." He lowered his voice to a whisper, and thanks to the influence of the ricebeer he made "Thorrburn" sound like it had several extra "r's." "Remember? You explained it to me." His eyes took on a familiar spark as he continued. "It worked. He knew what the starting gate was without having to be trained, as if he remembered it. And the first time he heard the bugle for the call to post..."

122

Deja Vu

"Are you arrogant enough to think you'll get away with it? You know that research into cloning is banned. And you've gone one step further. That makes it worse."

"Who's going to know?" His tone oozed defiance.

"*I* know," I muttered, swaying slightly as I stood to leave. I turned to him, mustering a stern expression.

"What if I made you a deal?" he said softly.

I plunked back into my chair and listened.

...

That's how I ended up with Maxx II. He's an exact replica of a Border Collie I had when I was in university—smartest, quirkiest dog I've ever known.

Maxx II was worth my silence—that, and the fact that my winnings allowed me to move into swankier digs. Just in time. That daily walking commute was starting to give me the creeps.

Maxx II was only possible because I knew where the bodies were buried. Well, the original Maxx's body anyway.

I never did find out where Luke got hold of Man O' War's DNA. I didn't need to know.

After Luke delivered Max II, I pleaded with him to be careful. "You don't know what kind of resources the Crime Syndicates have available," I warned. "There are all kinds of people who would be interested in your research. You need to lay low."

...

Luke excelled at lots of things, but laying low wasn't one of them.

If you follow the news at all, you know what happened six months later. Oh, the media tried to keep it hush-hush, but you can't keep a lid on something like that.

Someone besides me figured out Luke's little secret, and they tracked him down. They got the formula out of him, just before he died. The state his body was in spoke volumes about the amount of pain he'd endured before reluctantly yielding the information.

It's Come to Our Attention

Whoever captured Luke wasted no time. Combining Luke's forbidden knowledge with Quik-Gro, a technology originally patented for farm animals and supposedly banned on humans, they've brought back some of the most dreaded names from the history books.

In New York, there've been sightings of Varco Marbora, the man who sparked the genocides of the 2040's. In Los Angeles, there's video surveillance footage of Herbro Vincenza. Yeah, he's the guy who sold the results of his experiments with biochemical agents on the deep web in 2052. Social media has it that Attila the Hun or a close enough relative that only his mother could tell the difference has been spotted in the steppes of Australasia.

As for the "good guys," moral issues prevent them from bringing back the Einsteins and Ghandis and Kennedys, and—we may differ on the *who,* but the point is, they're not even trying. I don't like our odds, in the long run. Morality has its downside when it comes to combating people who aren't afraid to fight dirty.

I feel responsible, in a way. I can't help thinking that if I'd told the right people about Luke's little stunt back when it happened, and he'd gone to jail or had his memory wiped, this whole thing could have been avoided.

Plus, he'd still be here.

There's a saying that regret is a wasted emotion. My rational mind agrees.

Another part of me, the part that remembers Luke's laughing irreverence in Wykopf's genetics class, feels his loss. Deeply.

...

I didn't even hear a knock on the door. Perhaps there wasn't one. Maxx III was already there, barking like a Varcorian wolf dog, his teeth showing. Maxx III had cost me a ridiculous proportion of the stash that remained from my Derby winnings, but when the Maxx that Luke had created for me collapsed and died in my arms a few months after he was "born," I felt compelled to replace him with a dog that came into the world the customary way.

The hair on Maxx III's back raised into a stiff ridge as a growl rumbled deep in his throat.

"Easy, boy," I said, padding to the door and patting his head.

"It's me," a voice said from the other side of the door. "Open up."

It was a familiar voice. It was a voice that I shouldn't be hearing.

Have I mentioned that I am insatiably curious? Against my better judgment, I opened the door.

"Let me in, quickly," the person at the door pleaded. He *looked* like Luke, albeit slightly thinner than the last time I'd seen him, but how could it be? "And pick your jaw up off the floor."

I stood aside to let him pass and slammed the door behind him.

"Thanks," he panted, glancing around the room. "I have a proposition for you, but you need to pack. Quickly."

I folded my arms in front of my chest. "I'm not going anywhere without an explanation."

"Fine. Here's the short version," his grin was more of a grimace. "I thought about what you said, told some people what I'd been up to. They used that knowledge to set a trap. Obviously," now his facial features shaped themselves into a genuine smile, "it wasn't really me that the people the trap was set for caught up with."

"Obviously," I commented, my voice dry.

"They got the formula, but it won't do them much good," he whispered. "The constructs don't last. I knew that when DarbyKing's health started to fail, shortly after the race."

Maxx III, having now decided our visitor wasn't so bad after all, stuck his muzzle into Luke's left hand and nudged it.

"I'm sorry," I said quickly, sensing how much the loss of the horse still pained him. "Maxx II died too. I thought he'd just caught a bug or something. . . "

"I apologize for that. I didn't know, honestly," Luke put his right hand on my arm, briefly. "Anyway, I may have slipped up. Someone's been following me the past few days. I need to get out of here." He walked over to the window, and peered out.

"Where?" I asked.

"Government needs help on one of the Frontier planets," he grunted. "I've been promised a new identity and a full lab to work with. I'd like you to come with me." He paused, and his tone softened. "I realized, when I saw you in the bar, how much I've missed you."

Something clicked then, at the back of my brain.

"You weren't as scatter-brained as you pretended to be, back in Wykopf's class, were you?" I asked.

"No," he confessed. "I figured you thought I was a spoiled rich kid. Didn't expect you to give me the time of day. Getting you to 'help' me seemed a good excuse to spend time together."

I smacked his arm, harder than I meant to, my anger at being manipulated warring with a sudden fierce joy. I thought about the life I'd led since leaving the rat race. Truth was, I had to confess to being bored. A change of scenery would be welcome.

"Under one condition," I said.

"Name it," he grinned.

"Maxx III has to come along."

"Wouldn't dream of leaving him."

"Well, Maxx," I turned to the dog. "Let's get packed."

Deja Vu

Maxx III was way ahead of me. He already had his leash in his mouth.

Smart dog.

About the Author

Lisa Timpf is a freelance writer who resides in Simcoe, Ontario. Her work has appeared in a variety of venues, including *The Martian Wave, Outposts of Beyond, New Myths,* and *Scifaikuest.*

*****~~~~*****

Credits and Acknowledgments

Illustrations

Cover image and design – Keely Rew

Ebook Only:

Ice-Cold – English pub. Author: Sung Kuk Kim, All Rights Reserved. www.bikeworldtravel.com, commons.wikimedia.org

The Translator – "His Master's Voice," Artist: Francis Barraud, 1898, public domain, commons.wikimedia.org

Readers

Andrew Cairns, Tom Parker, Keely Rew

*****~~~~*****

It's Come to Our Attention
Discover other titles by Third Flatiron:

(1) Over the Brink: Tales of Environmental Disaster

(2) A High Shrill Thump: War Stories

(3) Origins: Colliding Causalities

(4) Universe Horribilis

(5) Playing with Fire

(6) Lost Worlds, Retraced

(7) Redshifted: Martian Stories

(8) Astronomical Odds

(9) Master Minds

(10) Abbreviated Epics

(11) The Time It Happened

(12) Only Disconnect

(13) Ain't Superstitious

(14) Third Flatiron's Best of 2015

www.thirdflatiron.com

THIRD FLATIRON